FINDERS WEEPERS

FINDERS WEEPERS

M I R I A M   C H A I K I N

drawings by RICHARD EGIELSKI

HARPER & ROW, PUBLISHERS

NEW YORK

Cambridge
Hagerstown
Philadelphia
San Francisco

London
Mexico City
São Paulo
Sydney

1817

Finders Weepers

Text copyright © 1980 by Miriam Chaikin
Illustrations copyright © 1980 by Richard Egielski

FIRST EDITION

Library of Congress Cataloging in Publication Data
Chaikin, Miriam.
 Finders weepers.

 SUMMARY: Molly finds a ring in the street that
causes her more problems than she could have
imagined.
 [1. Jews in the United States—Fiction.
2. Family life—Fiction] I. Egielski, Richard.
II. Title.
PZ7.C3487Fi 1980   [Fic]   79-9608
ISBN 0-06-021176-8
ISBN 0-06-021177-6 (lib. bdg.)

For Bennie,
and the clan in the desert.

CONTENTS

1

"SMILE, EVERYONE!"

Molly looked at the dress with disgust. The whole of P.S. 164 would laugh at her, if they could see her in it.

"I'm not going to wear it, and that's all," Molly said.

Mama stood facing her, holding up a brown taffeta dress with puffed sleeves, Molly's most recent hand-me-down from the rich cousins. Later, at three o'clock, the family had an appointment with Mr. Siegel, the photographer. Every year for Rosh Hashana, the Jewish New Year, Mama sent her brother in Palestine a family picture. And she wanted Molly to pose wearing the brown taffeta dress.

"Why can't I wear my dusty-pink dress?" Molly asked.

"It's too tight for you," her mother said. "This fits, and it's beautiful."

Molly looked at her mother. "Beautiful? It's ugly!" she said.

Mama turned toward the kitchen. "Everyone!" she called, summoning the rest of the family to come into the bedroom Molly shared with Rebecca, her little sister.

Rebecca came in, sucking on the rag that was always in her mouth. Joey followed, then Papa, with Yaaki in his arms.

Mama held up the dress. "Look," she said. "Isn't it beautiful? And she doesn't want to wear it for the picture."

"It's for a party," Rebecca said, talking through the rag in her mouth.

"See?" Molly gave her sister a grateful glance. "She's only a little kid, and even she knows it stinks."

"Molly! Watch your language," Mama said.

"What's wrong with stink?" Molly said. "It means smell. The dress was in the trunk the whole summer. It st— smells of camphor."

Rebecca had taken the rag out of her mouth. "I'm not a little kid, I'm four," she said.

"Come on, Molly, don't be like that," Mama said, holding the dress up admiringly.

Yaaki began to cry and Papa rocked him. "What's so hard?" Papa said. "It's only for a few minutes, Molly. You'll put it on when we go, and take it off when we come back."

"Boy!" Joey, Molly's older brother, said. "What's the big deal? I never saw anything like it. Did you see what I have to wear? My winter *Shabbos* suit, on a hot day like this! Do you think I want to? It's for the picture."

Molly puckered her lips and kissed the air. "You're a regular angel," she said.

"You're a spoiled brat," Joey said.

Mama patted the dress. "She's not spoiled. She's going to wear it. Aren't you, Molly?"

Molly could have spit. Taking the picture was bad enough. She hated the idea of trooping through the street in the middle of the day, all dressed up. To have to wear that ugly dress on top of it was just too much.

"Ma," she said firmly. "If I have to wear that dress, I'm not going to be in the picture."

"If that's how you're going to act," Mama said, "then Joey can take the skates today!"

Molly was shocked. This was her day for the skates. She and Tsippi were supposed to go skating this afternoon. "Ma!" she cried.

"Thanks, Ma," Joey said almost in the same breath. "I'll just go finish my homework," he added as he left the room.

Mama hung the dress up in front of the open window. "Let it airy out," she said in a flat voice. "The smell will go away."

Mama and Papa left the room. Rebecca got the wooden duck from under the bureau and pulled it along after herself as she left. Molly didn't want anyone to see the tears in her eyes. She took her library book and went into the living room with it. She sat down on the couch. The book was *Treasure Island*, but she couldn't read it. Her thoughts were on the skates. She could get them back, if she went in and apologized. But she did not want to do that. She wanted her mother to change her mind.

Molly pretended to be reading, but she sat listening to the sounds in the kitchen. Yaaki was banging on his high chair with a spoon. She heard her mother say something about shortening an old dress of Molly's, for Rebecca to wear in the picture.

"Laya," she heard her father say, "you're standing near the radio; turn it on. The news will be on soon."

They act as if nothing happened, Molly thought angrily.

A radio announcer came on saying that the German army was now deeper in Russia. Then the voice of a Washington Senator was telling America not to help Russia fight the Nazis. The announcer's voice came back saying there were reports that all the Jews in a town in Latvia had been killed by the Nazis.

Papa cursed. "Jews are being killed, and nobody lifts a finger to help," he said.

"It's heartbroking," Mama said.

"Heart*breaking*," Molly heard Joey say, correcting her.

Molly turned the page as if she were reading. She felt ashamed, worrying about skates when Jews were being killed in Europe. She thought of Hanna Gittel, in her Hebrew school. Hanna Gittel was younger. But Molly couldn't help noticing her, with her funny haircut. She was a refugee. Hitler had killed her father. But she and her mother had escaped from Europe.

After the news, Papa came into the living room and sat down in the easy chair to read his Yiddish paper. Molly saw Joey go to the kitchen closet where the skates were kept. As if it were his day for skates, he took them and went to the door.

That was that! Molly hadn't apologized. And Mama hadn't changed her mind about the skates. Molly blinked away some tears.

"I'm going," she heard him call to Mama.

"Salad," Mama said.

"What?" Joey asked.

"Salad," Mama repeated.

"What's salad?" Joey asked.

"Salad! Salad!" Mama said, exasperated. "Don't you understand English? Your friends say it all the time. Molly's friends too."

Joey laughed. "Not salad, Ma. *Solid!*" he said, and ran out.

Molly had to smile to herself. Her mother liked to use American expressions, but she never got them right.

The baby came crawling rapidly into the living room and Mama rushed in after him and scooped him up in her arms. His crib stood alongside Papa's chair, and he laughed as she put him into it.

He stood rattling the sides of the crib, making little yelling noises. Molly looked at her little brother, his blond curls bouncing. It made her feel good to see him that way. He had asthma, and was sick so much of the time.

Papa's voice came from behind the newspaper. "Molly, it says here your Hebrew school is having a parade tomorrow evening. Are you marching in it?"

Molly and Joey went to Hebrew school every Sunday morning. Joey went more often. He was older and preparing for his Bar Mitzvah. Molly was willing enough to learn to read and write Hebrew. But she didn't care for the extra things, like marching in parades or being in plays. Most of the kids who did those things seemed like drips to her. A lot of them were refugees. They came from the Other Side. Some could hardly speak English.

"I don't like to march in parades," she said. "I just want to be a plain American girl, playing with my own friends."

Papa lowered his paper and glared at her.

"What does that mean, young lady? Are you ashamed of being Jewish?"

Molly flushed. That was not what she had meant at all. Because she was angry, her thought had come out all wrong.

"Hitler is killing Jews in Europe," Papa continued,

"and my daughter talks about being a plain American girl. You're a Jewish American girl, not a plain American. Are we going to have another Selma-the-Communist in the family?"

"Pa!" Molly cried, resenting being compared to her cousin Selma-the-Communist.

"What do you mean, 'Pa'?" he asked.

Molly felt terrible. She looked from her father to her mother. She saw the hurt in their eyes. Suddenly the skates and the dress were unimportant. She only wanted everything to be nice again.

"I'm not in the parade, but I am going to watch," she said, hoping her sudden decision would improve the mood in the room. "Are you going, Pa?" she asked.

Her father lowered his paper. "It's after work. I can go," he said.

"If it's nice, I'll take the baby, and we'll all go," Mama said. The baby began to whimper and she went over to feel his diaper, to see if it needed changing.

"MOLLY!" Tsippi's voice called from outside.

Just in time, Molly thought as she jumped up to open the window. She and Tsippi were best friends.

"Hi," Molly called.

Tsippi, on skates and wearing a skirt and sweater, pushed her glasses up on her nose. "You coming out?"

"My brother has the skates," Molly said in a loud voice, hoping to make her mother feel guilty.

"That's okay. Look, I'll lend you one of mine," Tsippi said. "We can hold on to each other and skate together."

Molly laughed. "Can we do that?"

"I don't know. Let's try," Tsippi said. "We'll skate over to Julie's house."

"I'll be right out," Molly said. She passed her mother in the kitchen. Mama was ironing the same old long-sleeved black dress with gold thread she wore in every picture. It smelled of camphor too.

"I'm going," Molly said, speaking through her nose so as not to have to smell the camphor.

Her mother looked up. "Don't forget the picture. We have to be by Mr. Siegel at three o'clock."

Molly walked to the door in silence, determined not to wear that dress.

"Tell Rebecca to come in; I'll clean her up," Mama called after her.

Tsippi was sitting on the bottom step of the stoop, wearing a skate on her right foot and holding one up to Molly. "Here, put it on your left foot."

Molly sat down to put it on. Rebecca came up to them. She looked at the skates, one on the foot of each girl. "That's dumb," she said.

"Nobody asked you," Molly said, tightening the clamps with a skate key. "Go inside. Mama wants you."

Molly stood up and scraped the ground with her left foot, setting the wheels spinning.

"Let's go," Tsippi said, getting to her feet and pushing her glasses up on her nose.

"How do we start?" Molly asked with a giggle.

Tsippi walked around to the other side of Molly, so that each girl had a skate on an outside foot. "We hold up the empty foot, and skate like we had one body." She put an arm around Molly.

Molly put her arm around Tsippi. "Okay. Let's go."

When they each lifted a skateless foot and tried to move, they burst out laughing as they nearly fell over.

Rebecca began to laugh too. Molly looked at her sister. Rebecca hardly ever laughed. "What are you waiting for?" Molly asked.

Rebecca held on to the railing and went up the steps.

Molly and Tsippi tried but couldn't get going without falling over each other. In the end, they decided to take the skates off and walk. As they headed for Thirteenth Avenue, Molly told Tsippi about the argument at home. Then they discussed the geography homework Miss McCabe had given them: to make a list of the products America imported from South America.

"I'll come to your house after supper, and we can do it together," Tsippi said. "My father said I could. My stepmother too."

Molly was delighted. "Then we can listen to the radio," she said. "Sunday is the best night. Eddie Cantor is on, and Charlie McCarthy, and Baby Snooks."

As they passed the courtyard of the Hebrew school, Molly saw Hanna Gittel playing ball against the wall with some girls. She remembered how scared Hanna Gittel used to be when she first came. She never looked up or talked to anyone. She still looked like a greenhorn, with her short hair and funny clothes. But now she laughed and ran around like everybody else. And even though she still spoke with an accent, her English was getting better.

"Hi, Molly," Hanna Gittel called.

Molly waved back. "She's in my class in Hebrew school," she told Tsippi.

"I wish I could go to Hebrew school too, and learn Hebrew," Tsippi said. "But my father wants me to learn Yiddish. I don't want to."

Molly was surprised. So far as she knew, only refugees spoke Yiddish. They tried to learn English, not the other way around.

The girls made their way among the shoppers crowding the pushcarts on Thirteenth Avenue, and rang Julie's bell. She lived above the tailor store. The girls looked up at her window.

"Hi," Julie called down. "I'm not ready yet. But my mother said I could go out. Come up, okay?" she added.

The girls glanced at each other. They hated to go up to Julie's house. Her mother was a pill. But they didn't want to hurt Julie's feelings. They nodded to her, then climbed the stairs.

Julie was at the sink washing dishes when they came in.

"It won't take long," Julie said, blowing her frizzy red hair out of her eyes.

"Who came in?" Mrs. Roth's voice called from the living room.

"Molly and Tsippi," Julie answered, taking a towel and drying.

Mrs. Roth shuffled into the kitchen wearing a man's bathrobe and slippers and holding a rag to her head.

"How do you feel today, Mrs. Roth?" Molly asked, just to be polite.

"Not too well. My head hurts," Mrs. Roth answered.

Molly and Tsippi glanced at each other. They had discussed it often. Mrs. Roth only pretended to be sick, so

Julie would feel sorry for her and stay home with her. Mr. Roth ran away with another woman when Julie was little, and Mrs. Roth had been that way ever since.

Mrs. Roth touched Tsippi's skates. "Some kids have everything," she said.

Tsippi blushed and looked away.

"Your mothers are lucky," Mrs. Roth said, turning to Molly. "They have husbands to help them raise their children."

Molly tried to smile but couldn't.

Mrs. Roth held the rag under the cold water, then squeezed it and put it back on her forehead. "Ohhhhh," she moaned, and shuffled back into the living room.

The moan gave Molly the shivers. No wonder people said Julie was nervous. Who wouldn't be, living with that sound? Molly thought of her own mother and felt guilty. Sometimes she was ashamed of her mother because she didn't speak English well and because she wore old-fashioned clothes. Mrs. Roth was born in America and spoke English perfectly. But she was awful. Molly wondered if Julie loved her mother. She decided she was lucky to have the mother she had. And she suddenly decided to wear the taffeta dress after all.

Julie was finished drying. "She'll put them away," she said, blowing the hair out of her eyes. She turned toward the living room. "I'm going," she called inside.

"Take thirty-five cents from the money and get salami and baked beans for supper," Mrs. Roth called back.

Julie took some coins from under a dish in the china closet.

"Don't lose the money," Mrs. Roth called as they went down the stairs.

The girls walked around on Thirteenth Avenue for a while. Then they sat on the running board of a parked car and talked about the Bette Davis movie they had seen. Next to reading books, Molly liked Bette Davis movies best. She wore her hair in bangs, to copy Bette Davis.

"*Oooo*," Molly said, noticing that the clock on the bank read nearly 2. "I better get home."

"Why?" Julie asked.

Molly made a face. "To take a family picture to send to my uncle in Palestine."

"I wish I had an uncle," Julie said.

Molly laughed. "What good is it? He lives in Palestine. I never saw him."

"I wouldn't care where he lived," Julie said. "I just wish I had an uncle—someplace."

Molly turned to Tsippi. "See you later," she said. She felt funny, not including Julie. She knew Julie's mother didn't let her go out after supper. Still, she felt she ought to say something. "Tsippi's coming over later to do homework and listen to the radio. Want to come?"

Julie shrugged. "I'll ask my mother."

" 'Bye," Molly called over her shoulder and ran off.

She thought of Hanna Gittel as she turned the corner. Molly wondered what it was like to be a refugee. Even the word was awful. A picture of Hanna Gittel running away from Hitler came to her mind and she shuddered.

Something shiny on the ground caught her eye and she bent to pick it up. It was a beautiful gold ring. She thought immediately of Bette Davis, her favorite actress. In the movie she had seen, Bette Davis wore a gold ring on her left pinky. And every time George Brent came near her she began to twist and turn it.

Molly tried the ring on the same finger. It wouldn't turn—it was too tight—but she loved the way it looked. She took it off and put it in her pocket. Her mother would never allow her to wear it because it didn't belong to her. She would make her look for the owner. But Molly did not want to look for the owner. She wanted to keep the ring. She knew she would think of something as she ran home.

When she walked into the kitchen she found everyone all dressed up and seated around the table. They stared at her.

"What are you looking at me like that for?" she asked.

"Like what?" Joey said. "The door opened. We looked. It was you."

"I'll be ready in a minute," she said, and ran into her room. She put her ring in the sock drawer, which Rebecca couldn't reach. Then she went to the closet. She looked lovingly at the dusty-pink dress. But her mother was right. It was too tight on her. Grudgingly, she took the brown taffeta off the hanger. She stepped into the closet for privacy, and got dressed.

When she came out of the closet, everyone was standing around looking at her.

Mama clapped her hands. "You look beautiful," she said.

"You do look nice," Joey said, adding quickly, "from the back."

"Jo-ey!" Mama said. "Don't start up now."

Molly glanced at herself in the mirror. She was a

stranger to herself, all dressed up in that dumb dress! As her anger came swimming back, she thought of Julie's mother and reminded herself that she only had to wear it until the picture had been taken.

"Do I look nice too?" Rebecca asked.

"Beautiful," Mama said. She gave Rebecca a long look. "Did you go to the bathroom?"

"I don't have to," Rebecca said.

Papa looked at Mama. "Is she sure?"

"Are you sure?" Mama asked.

Rebecca nodded and stuck the rag in her mouth.

"Leave that here—so the duck won't be lonely," Mama said.

"All right," Rebecca said. She put the rag on her wooden duck, which sat on the floor in the corner, and got her little pink plastic doll with the dented belly instead.

Mama lifted the baby out of the crib and gave him to Papa to hold. "Let's go," she said.

Outside, Joey and Papa walked in front, with the baby. Mama and Rebecca walked behind them. And Molly walked in back, alone. Even outdoors, the camphor smelled to high heaven. She was glad none of her friends were around to see her in her taffeta dress, or smell it.

Mr. Siegel dropped a curtain behind a red velvet bench. He sat Mama and Papa on the bench and put the baby in Papa's arms. He stood Molly alongside of Papa, and placed Rebecca in front of her. Joey was moved to the other side of the bench, next to Mama.

When Mr. Siegel had them all where he wanted them,

he ran to the front of the room and stuck his head under a cloth that covered the camera.

"Don't be so serious, everybody," he said from under the cloth. "Nobody is going to bite you."

Then he came rushing out to put Molly's hand on Papa's shoulder, and move Rebecca closer to Molly. He disappeared back under the cloth.

Rebecca was standing on Molly's foot and she shoved her forward.

"Stop!" Rebecca said.

Molly stared down at the part in her sister's hair and said nothing. The less that was said, the sooner the picture would be over.

"Beautiful children, all of them," Mr. Siegel said from under the cloth. "But I never saw a beauty like the baby."

"All the boys in our family are beautiful," Joey said.

"Hmmph!" said Molly.

"He has asthma," Rebecca said.

"Nobody move," Mr. Siegel's voice called.

"Ma, I have to go to the bathroom," Rebecca said.

"*Nu! Nu!*" Mama said, staring straight ahead.

"You see—?" Papa said, without turning his head.

"Can you hold it in?" Mama asked.

"I don't know," Rebecca said.

"Try," Mama said.

"Smile, everyone!" Mr. Siegel said as his hand reached up for the rubber bulb that snapped the picture.

Molly squished her eyes together, hoping it looked like a smile.

"The older girl, can you smile a little more, please?" Mr. Siegel's voice asked.

Molly tried.

"A little more," he called.

"Eeeee!" Molly cried, feeling a warm stream on her foot.

"Perfect!" Mr. Siegel said, squeezing the rubber bulb and sending a puff of smoke up into the air.

2

GEOGRAPHY

In the morning Yaaki started to cough again, and Mama kept running between the crib in the living room and the breakfast table in the kitchen. Molly buttered a roll for herself. She was sorry Yaaki was sick. But she was just as glad Mama was busy.

Molly had not said anything about the ring, and she couldn't bring herself to look her mother in the eye. The ring was in the drawer. Earlier, when Rebecca was out of the room, Molly had put it on. But she couldn't figure out what to say that would allow her mother to let her keep it. So she piled the socks up over it and left it in the drawer until she could think of something.

"Pass the milk," Joey said.

Molly helped herself to some more milk, then passed the bottle.

Rebecca, still in her pajamas, came out of the bathroom and sat down at the table to drink the Ovaltine Mama had prepared for her. Molly passed her the jelly, to have with her roll.

At the sound of the doorbell, Molly gulped down her milk and got up. That was Tsippi, coming to call for her. Tsippi walked a whole block out of her way each morning just to call for Molly, so they could walk to school together. "I gotta go," Molly called as she put her dirty glass in the sink. She got into her sweater, took up her school bag, and ran out the door.

"Hi," she said, running down the steps.

Tsippi was all bundled up in a sweater and coat. She pushed her glasses back up on her nose. "Look what my stepmother made me wear," she said. "She acts like we live at the North Pole."

As they walked to school together, Molly talked about the Baby Snooks program they had listened to last night, and about the Hebrew school parade she was supposed to go to after school. She talked about everything except the ring. Somehow, she felt guilty about it. This was the first secret she had ever kept from Tsippi. She would have liked to tell her, but was afraid to take the chance. What if Tsippi knew the person who had lost it? The ring would have to be given back.

It was early when they arrived at the school yard. The starting bell hadn't rung yet, and Providence and Augie and some of the big kids in Molly's class were playing ball. Molly and Tsippi stopped to watch. Soon Big and Little Naomi came up to them, and they went off to one side and stood talking.

"Hi, Molly," Julie called.

Molly looked up. Julie used the boys' entrance. It was closest to her house. "Hi," she called back. She motioned to Julie to come over, but Julie shook her head and went inside. She liked to be early.

Tsippi pulled Molly by the sleeve. "There's Beverly," she said.

"Don't let her see us," Molly said, turning away.

Molly sat next to Beverly, in the front row. She

couldn't stand Beverly. But because they were the two smallest kids in the class, they were always being seated together.

"Let's go," Little Naomi said, pulling Big Naomi by the sleeve.

"It's early yet," Big Naomi said.

"I'm going," Little Naomi said and walked off. Big Naomi followed.

"That Little Naomi is so bossy," Molly said.

"I know it," Tsippi said. "I guess we should go in too."

The girls went up the staircase to the next floor. Miss McCabe was sitting at her desk reading the paper. She seated children according to size, and Molly went to her seat in the front row and Tsippi to hers in a middle row. Miss McCabe looked up at Molly with a smile and Molly smiled back. She liked the teacher, even though she sometimes picked on her. Just as the starting bell rang, Providence and Augie ran in. They sat in back, with the other giants.

Miss McCabe folded her paper, put it in her bottom drawer, and got up.

"All right," she said, walking to the window side of the room. "Let's begin." She looked around at the class. "Will the first one in each row collect the homework and take it to my desk?"

Molly detached her homework assignment from her book, then walked up the aisle and took everyone's sheet to Miss McCabe's desk. She went to her seat again.

Beverly moved over on her seat and came closer to Molly. "Miss McCabe has a run in her stocking," she whispered.

Walking over to the center window where she liked to stand, Miss McCabe glanced over her shoulder. "That'll do," she said, giving Molly the eye. Molly could have killed Beverly. She knew just when to glance away, so it would look like someone else had done the talking. Molly made an angry face at her and turned to Miss McCabe, standing with her arms crossed in front of the window.

"What is the capital of Peru?" Miss McCabe asked.

Molly couldn't think of the answer and quickly lowered her head. She couldn't imagine why Miss McCabe was asking for capitals. Products had been the class homework, not capitals.

"Molly!" Miss McCabe called.

Molly looked up, surprised. Miss McCabe must be trying to get even with her. She knew Molly would have raised her hand if she had known the answer.

"Stand up, please," Miss McCabe said.

Resentfully, Molly stood up. She tried to remember the answer. She had known it only a few days ago. It had to still be in her head someplace.

"The capital of Peru . . ." she began, speaking slowly.

"Well . . . ?" Miss McCabe said.

Molly noticed Beverly's lips twitching and looked away. Beverly always pretended to be helping with an answer, but she never knew what she was talking about.

Molly almost had the answer. It was on the tip of her tongue. "The capital of Peru," she began again, reaching for it in her mind. The answer sounded like a person's name. But who? Mama's Aunt Lena. That was it!

"Lima!"

"Cor-rect," Miss McCabe said.

Relieved, Molly sat down. Now she could breathe easily. Miss McCabe never called on the same person twice. She sat back and let her thoughts wander, and found herself thinking about the ring. She pictured herself wearing it, and saw her friends gathering around to admire it. What if she wore the ring to school and some girl there said she had lost it?

"The mountains of Peru, what are they called? Beverly!" Miss McCabe said.

Beverly stood up and chewed on her lips as if she were trying to remember, until Miss McCabe told her to sit down again.

Molly covered her mouth to keep from laughing and glanced over her shoulder at Tsippi.

"Raymond!"

"The Andes," Raymond said, half rising in his seat.

"Cor-rect."

Miss McCabe returned to the front of the room where a rolled-up map hung on the wall, over the blackboard. She took up the pointer and pulled down the map.

"This is a map of South America," she said. "And this is Peru." She stabbed the orange blob on the map with the pointer.

"What products does Peru export? Call out from your seats if you know the answer."

"Gold," Raymond called.

"Silver," Tsippi's voice answered.

"Lead," Molly added, remembering her homework.

"Cor-rect."

Molly felt good about having given the right answer, and glanced at Beverly, hoping to see some sign of approval, but Beverly had turned away and stuck her nose in her book, as if she were reading.

Suddenly the classroom door opened and Mr. Brooke, the principal, came in.

Molly froze. Was she seeing things? He was carrying Rebecca in his arms! Rebecca sat looking calmly about, sucking on her rag. Alarmed, Molly wondered what it meant. Had Rebecca been run over? Was something wrong at home? Had Mama sent her to school to get Molly?

Mr. Brooke spoke briefly to Miss McCabe, then turned to the class. "Is anybody here this little girl's sister? She won't give her name, or her sister's, but she says her sister attends this school."

Molly was furious. Nothing was wrong at home! It wasn't anything important at all. Rebecca had just taken it into her head to come to school. "She's my sister," Molly said, embarrassed.

Mr. Brooke put Rebecca down. "Would you take her home, please? Your mother will be worrying."

Molly went up to the front of the room and took Rebecca by the hand.

"Take her home, then come back," Miss McCabe said. "And watch yourself at the corner. There are no monitors out now."

Blushing, Molly led her sister out of the room and down the hall. She was walking too fast, she knew, but she didn't care. She pulled Rebecca along to the end of the hall, then down the stairs, and past the principal's office.

The bulletin board next to the principal's office gave Molly an idea. It was used for lost-and-found notices, and Molly stopped to look at it. There was one notice, about a teachers' meeting. Nothing about a lost ring. Molly drew a deep breath. At least the person who had lost the ring probably didn't go to P.S. 164. She could wear the ring freely. Now all she had to do was persuade her mother.

Rebecca became impatient and tried to wriggle out of her grasp, and Molly took a firm hold of her hand and led her out of the building.

Outside in the school yard, she dropped her sister's hand. "Why did you come here?" she asked, looking daggers at Rebecca.

Rebecca took the blanket out of her mouth to answer. "I want to go to school," she said.

Her answer only made Molly angrier. "Look what you did, you rotten kid. You made me miss geography. You embarrassed me in front of the whole class. Why didn't you go to Joey's school, and embarrass him?" Instantly, Molly regretted her words. Joey's school was two blocks away, across two big gutters. What if Rebecca did decide to go there? What if she got run over? Or kidnapped? It would all be Molly's fault.

"I want to go to school, too," Rebecca repeated. "I want to hold someone's hand and stand in line." Tears were beginning to form in her eyes.

Molly hated to see her sister cry. She took her hand. "You're holding my hand," she said more softly, as she led her across the school yard.

"No," Rebecca said. "You're my sister. That doesn't count. I want a real person, from my class," she added, and started to cry.

"I told you a hundred times," Molly said gently, "you're too young to go to school."

"Then when can I go?" Rebecca asked, her eyes full of tears.

"Next year."

"When is next year?"

"Soon."

"When is soon?"

"Winter comes, then spring, then summer. After that."

They paused at the corner and looked to see that no cars were coming, then hurried across the street.

Mama was scrubbing clothes in the kitchen sink when they came in. A worried expression crossed her face as she looked up and saw them. She wiped her hands on her apron and came running. "Molly, what are you doing home from school?"

Molly flung Rebecca's hand away. "Guess," she said.

Mama glanced from one to the other. "What happened?"

"Your child," Molly said, glaring at Rebecca, "came to school all by herself. The principal found her and took her to all the classes. She wouldn't tell her name, or her sister's. Ma, I was so embarrassed!"

Mama touched her cheek in surprise. She looked at Rebecca. "You crossed alone? The big gutter?"

"I asked a man to cross me," Rebecca said.

"A stranger?"

"He works in the drugstore," Rebecca said.

"Don't you care what happened to *me*?" Molly asked.

"I know you can cross yourself," Mama said.

"I don't mean about that. I mean about school. Look

how she embarrassed me. And she made me miss geography too."

Mama looked up. "Next to Tsippi, you're best in geography, you told me yourself. You can afford to miss a few minutes, nothing terrible will happen."

"Tsippi is best, then Raymond, *then* me," Molly said.

"Excuse me for leaving," Mama said.

"Living," said Molly, correcting her.

Mama sat down and took Rebecca into her arms. "Rebecca, I thought you were next door, with Mrs. Chiodo. Why did you go away without telling me?"

"I was afraid of the doctor," Rebecca said.

"What doctor?" Molly asked.

"The baby started coughing. He couldn't catch his breath. I had to call Dr. Pearl," Mama said. "He came right away."

Molly hurried into the living room. The baby was making gurgling noises and kicking his feet. "*Kootsie-koo*," she said, catching a foot and giving it a squeeze. He gave her a smile, showing two tiny white teeth.

"He's better now," Mama called.

"What did the doctor say?" Molly asked, coming back into the kitchen.

Mama got up. "He gave him some medicine, and the coughing stopped." She took a slip of paper from the top of the icebox and gave it to Molly.

"He gave a prescription. Leave it with the druggist, and pick up the medicine when you come home for lunch."

"LA-YA," Mrs. Baumfeld called from the courtyard.

Mama went to the window.

"Your husband called. He said he has to work late. He can't go to the parade."

Molly heard. She had forgotten about the parade.

"Thank you, Goldie," Mama said.

"I'm going shopping. You need something?"

"No, thanks," Mama said, and turned back to the room. "God bless her and her telephone," she added. She looked at Molly. "I can't go to the parade either. The baby is not well. Also, it's Rosh Hashanah in two days. Bessie and Heshy are coming. And Esther, and the children."

Children! Molly thought, thinking of her cousin Selma. Selma was ancient. She was sixteen.

"I have to start cleaning the house for the new year. I want to put new papers in the drawers," she added.

Molly's heart turned over. "I like to do drawers," she said quickly. "I didn't want to go to the parade anyhow. I'll help you when I come home."

"Fine," Mama said.

"What about the parade?" Rebecca asked.

"Nobody's going," Molly said.

"But I want to go," Rebecca said.

"Maybe Mrs. Chiodo will take you," Mama said.

"She's not Jewish," Rebecca said.

"You don't have to be Jewish to go to a parade," Mama said.

Molly started for the door. "I'm going," she said.

"I'm going too," Rebecca said, following.

Mama sat down on a kitchen chair and drew Rebecca toward her. "Why don't you stay home with me? We'll listen to the radio. Soon the good programs will be on. *Our Gal Sunday.* You like it."

[27]

Molly looked at her sister wonderingly. She wasn't like the other kids in the neighborhood. Her best friend was Mrs. Chiodo, the lady who lived next door. And she preferred listening to the radio with Mama to playing outside with her friends.

For an instant, Molly was jealous. She would have liked to stay home too. She liked sitting with Mama and Rebecca and listening to the radio. Next to reading and the movies, Molly liked listening to the radio best. It was like reading, the way it made pictures in her head.

"Ma, sometimes I think Rebecca is a midget, and not a little girl," Molly said.

Rebecca looked at Molly with an expressionless face.

"Come on, I'll give you," Mama said, patting Molly on the behind.

"Hey!" Molly said suddenly, reminding herself that she had to get back to school. "I have to go."

"Go already," Mama said. "I don't want the true officer coming to tell me you're playing hockey."

"Not true, Ma, *truant*. And it's not hockey, it's *hookey*," Molly said.

"So long as you know what I mean," Mama said. She took a banana from a bowl on the table, peeled it, and handed it to Rebecca.

Molly thought of the drawer. "You won't touch the drawers before I get home?" she said.

"Why should I? It's your job," Mama said. "Don't forget to leave the prescription," she added.

"I won't," Molly answered on her way out.

She wondered, as she walked to the drugstore, what she could say to her mother that would permit her to keep the ring. And as she left the drugstore and waited for the light to change she hit on a plan.

Later, when she was doing the drawers, she would put the ring under her pillow. In the morning, she would take it to school. Then, when she came home from school, she would tell her mother someone threw it out of a passing car and she found it in the gutter. The car was gone. Her mother couldn't expect her to find the owner of the ring.

She felt good, and skipped the rest of the way to school.

Miss McCabe glanced up as she entered the room.

". . . the mountains of Peru," Molly heard her say.

Still Peru! Molly thought as she took her seat. She was sick of Peru and could hardly wait to start on Switzerland, which they would be taking up next.

As she glanced over her shoulder, she was surprised to see that Tsippi wasn't in her seat.

"Where's Tsippi?" she whispered to Beverly.

"She was sick; she went home."

"Molly," Miss McCabe said as she rolled up the map, "while you were gone I decided it would be nice if we could all have lunch together tomorrow. Bring a lunch from home."

Molly liked bringing lunch to school. She hoped Tsippi would be back tomorrow so they could sit together.

Beverly leaned toward her as Miss McCabe turned her back to the class. "Did your mother yell at your sister?" she asked.

Molly did not want to get in Dutch with the teacher again. She shook her head and did not answer.

"That'll do, Molly!" Miss McCabe called out shrilly.

3

"WHAT NATURE MEANS TO ME"

Molly had finished eating breakfast and sat alone at the kitchen table. She was dressed in a sweater and her school-bag was at her feet. She was feeling sorry for herself. The ring was in her schoolbag and she was supposed to be happy today. But she wasn't.

When she had gotten up, her mother had announced that the grippe was going around. That's what Tsippi must have, Molly had thought when she heard it. She had been sure of it when Tsippi had failed to show up. But sad as she was for her friend, that was not what was bothering her. Mama was making her wear garlic to school. It was in a cheesecloth pouch attached to a string around her neck. Mama said she had to wear it. She said it kept germs away. Molly was sure she stank to high heaven. She did not want to leave for school.

Rebecca came in from the living room, dragging her duck behind her. A piece of cotton stuck out of her ear. She had woken with an earache and Mama had put drops in.

Rebecca walked up to her and sniffed. "I can't smell the garlic," she said.

Molly knew she was only trying to make her feel better, but it didn't help. "What do you know, you're only a child," she said. "Besides, you can stay home where nobody will smell you. I have to go to school. They'll make fun of me."

"You're still home?" Mama called from the living room, where she was changing the baby.

"No, it's my double," Molly said.

"If you're so worried about the smell, go outside and airy yourself out," Mama called.

Molly was on the verge of tears. She lifted the piece of cheesecloth that held the garlic, gave it an angry look, and shoved it under her blouse.

"This thing that you made is something they do in Europe, not in America," she said. "Nobody in my class will be wearing it. Nobody in the whole school. In the whole world. Only me!"

Mama came in carrying the baby on her hip. She sat him in the high chair and gave him a spoon to play with. It was his favorite toy but it didn't seem to interest him today.

"In Europe," Mama said, "they bury an onion in the backyard and spit three times. I learned about garlic right here in America. So don't be such a smartypins."

"Smarty*pants*, not pins," Molly said.

"Joey's wearing it, he went to school, he didn't complain," Mama said.

Molly hated being compared to her brother. "Oh, Joey's an angel from heaven. He's wonderful," she said. "He's the most—"

"That's enough," Mama interrupted. She went to the closet and took out a mixing bowl and the rolling pin. "I have to make noodles," she said.

The holidays were coming and she seemed to be cooking all the time. She cleared away one end of the table, folded a clean pillowcase over it, then spread some flour over it.

[31]

Molly glanced at the clock on the icebox. It was getting late. She couldn't sit there forever. She thought of Tsippi. Mama had said the grippe was an epidemic. That meant the grippe was catching. Molly wouldn't even be able to go and visit her friend. She missed her already.

She put the lunch Mama had prepared for her into her schoolbag and went to the door.

Rebecca was sitting at the table, watching Mama mix flour and eggs in a bowl.

"I'm going," Molly called.

"So go already!" Mama answered.

Molly opened the door and left.

Outside, she stood for a moment on the stoop, holding the garlic up to the air and waving it about. Then she put it back under her blouse again.

Solly came down the steps as she walked by his stoop. He and Joey were in the same class in junior high. Molly liked him. He treated her like a real person.

"Where's Tsippi?" he asked. "Doesn't she walk to school with you every day?"

Molly nodded. She felt good in the company of an older boy. "She has the grippe," she said.

"A lot of kids in my class have it too." Solly leaned over and inhaled loudly.

"Hey! What are you doing?" Molly asked.

"I just wondered if you were wearing one too." He pulled a piece of cheesecloth out from under his shirt. "Garlic! My mother says it keeps the grippe away. She made me wear it. Pugh!" he added, and tucked it back under his shirt.

The fact that Solly was wearing garlic made Molly feel

better. His mother was born in America, not in Europe like her mother. Even so, she couldn't bring herself to admit that she also was wearing it.

"Watch, I bet I'll be wearing it tomorrow too," she said, prepared to go that far but no farther.

Molly waved good-bye at the school yard entrance as Solly walked on up the street; then she went inside. The school yard was empty. Hoping she wasn't late, she ran up the steps.

The door to class was open and Miss M°Cabe sat reading the newspaper. Molly glanced around the room. Lots of seats were empty. Including Beverly's. Molly found herself minding the garlic less and less. From the smell in the room, she was sure everyone was wearing garlic. She wondered if Miss M°Cabe was too.

She noticed fractions on the blackboard and made a face. Arithmetic was bad enough, but fractions were awful.

A moment later the starting bell rang and Miss M°Cabe looked up. "We have a small class today," she said, folding her paper. "Seymour, close the door, please."

"Vinnie is door monitor this week," Seymour answered.

"But Vinnie is not in today."

Seymour looked around the room. "He must be sick."

"As I said, Seymour, close the door, please."

Seymour got up and closed the door.

Molly giggled. She reached into her schoolbag for the ring. She could put it on now. No one at school had lost it. No one could say it wasn't hers. The ring looked beautiful on her hand and she wished Tsippi were around to see it.

"Only a fraction of the class is here today," Miss

[33]

McCabe said, pulling her mouth over to the side in a smile, "so we will not take up fractions today."

Molly was glad. She smiled back so Miss McCabe would know her joke wasn't wasted.

"We'll do penmanship instead. We can all stand a little improvement there," Miss McCabe added. "Ten lines of up-and-down strokes, ten of circles." She walked over to the window side of the room.

Molly raised the lid of her desk and took out her pen and a piece of paper. Penmanship wasn't one of her favorite subjects either, but it was better than fractions. She found her inkwell dry and raised her hand.

"I have no ink," she said when Miss McCabe looked her way.

"Who's in charge of ink this week?" Miss McCabe asked.

"Me," Providence called from the back.

She loped over to the wardrobe where the big ink bottle was kept and filled Molly's inkwell.

Molly dipped her pen into the ink again and again, just so she could see the ring. Then she began her up-and-down strokes. She didn't have to concentrate to do them, so she let her thoughts wander. She could hardly wait for tomorrow. It was fun, having the relatives come for Rosh Hashanah. She looked forward to seeing her Aunt Bessie, but not her Uncle Heshy. They didn't sleep over. But Aunt Esther, Selma-the-Communist, and Mordi did. Everyone had to double up. Molly's mattress was put on the floor, for Joey and Mordi to sleep on. Molly, Aunt Esther, and Rebecca slept on the bedsprings. And Selma-the-Communist got Joey's room—all to herself.

"How come?" Molly always asked.

"Because she's a young lady, that's why," her mother always answered.

"Young lady?" Molly thought, finishing her last row of up-and-down strokes. Selma was old—she was sixteen!

Just at the last stroke, her penpoint got stuck in the paper and ink spattered all over the page. Molly quickly got her blotter out and blotted it up. Her paper was full of spots.

"Next time don't use so much ink," she heard Miss McCabe say.

Molly jumped. She had no idea Miss McCabe was standing over her.

"The up-and-down strokes should be *inside* the lines, not outside," Miss McCabe added, and walked on.

Molly turned her sheet over and started a row of circles.

She didn't like this day at all. It dragged on and on. Lunch in the classroom was boring too. The whole room smelled of bananas. Even Miss McCabe seemed sorry she had suggested that everyone bring lunch.

In the afternoon, she read the class a poem about trees, by Joyce Kilmer, and some other poems by Robert Frost about the seasons.

Molly hardly paid attention. She kept looking at the ring. She just wished *someone* were around to notice it. Even Beverly.

Miss McCabe finished another poem. She seemed to enjoy reading aloud.

"For homework," she said, "I'd like you to write a composition: 'What Nature Means to Me.' " Molly made a face. That was not going to be easy. Nature meant nothing to her.

When the bell rang at three, even Miss M{{c}}Cabe seemed relieved.

Molly knew just what she was going to say when she ran home.

"Ma, look what I found," she cried as she opened the door.

"Shhh, quiet. And don't jump," Mama said from the window, where she was hanging out clothes.

Molly knew from the smell in the kitchen and from the warning that a cake was baking in the oven and that her mother didn't want her to ruin it with a heavy step.

Mama turned back to the window. "If I don't see you, have a nice holiday, Mrs. Baumfeld," she called upstairs.

"Look what I found," Molly repeated more softly.

Mama dried her hands on her apron and looked at the ring. "Where did you get it?"

"I found it in the gutter," Molly said. "A car was passing, and it fell out." She shrugged. "Maybe somebody threw it out, I don't know. . . ." She gazed at the ring. "Isn't it beautiful, Ma?"

"A car?" Mama asked.

Molly nodded.

"Maybe somebody in your school lost it?"

"Ma, it fell out of a car, I told you." She looked at it. "Finders keepers," she added gaily.

"A teacher, maybe?"

"Ma, it's a child's ring, and it fell out of a car, and the car is gone."

"Even so, look on the lawston board."

"What board?" Molly asked.

"Where people say they lost something."

Molly laughed. "Lost and found," she said.

Mama looked at the ring again. "It's too tight," she said.

Molly silently agreed. The ring was too tight. But she didn't care. She breathed easier. Her mother had run out of questions, she could tell. The ring was officially hers now.

Joey came in from the living room, closing the door behind himself. Molly was surprised to see him. He usually got home after her.

"What are you doing home?" she asked.

"I never went back to school after lunch," he said. "The baby wouldn't stop crying. I stayed home to help Mama." He nodded toward the living room. "He's sleeping now."

"Was he coughing again?" Molly asked, worried.

Joey nodded. "If it doesn't stop, he might have to go to the hospital."

"Ptu! Ptu!" Mama said, spitting away the evil thought. "He won't have to go. You'll see. God will help."

Molly went into the living room to look at the baby. He was fast asleep. A little wheezing sound came from his throat. Even with his eyes closed, he looked beautiful, with his curls falling around his head on the pillow.

A feeling of love for him welled up in Molly. Molly looked heavenward, asking God to help the baby. Then she sat down on the couch near the crib. She decided her homework could wait. Right now, she felt like looking at her ring and listening to the radio.

Mama's favorite program, *Life Can Be Beautiful*, would be coming on soon.

She turned on the radio. It needed to warm up before it would play. She didn't have to worry about the noise waking the baby. The sound couldn't be heard unless someone held a loose wire in back. As the radio warmed, she could hear, faintly, faintly, the strains of "When You Wish Upon a Star" being sung. She hummed along, placing her hand this way and that, looking at the ring.

Then she heard her mother and brother arguing in the kitchen and looked up.

"I don't want it in the house, and that's all," Mama said.

Molly saw Joey go to the front door in a huff.

The baby started to wheeze again, and Mama came running into the living room. She straightened the blanket that he had kicked off and gently covered him. Then she turned the radio off, unplugged it, and took it into the kitchen. Molly followed, closing the door. Mama put the radio on the kitchen table.

"Ow!" Molly cried, stubbing her toe as she sat down at the table.

"Shhh," Mama said. "You'll wake the baby."

"I nearly broke my foot," Molly said. She bent down to look under the table, and there was a steel bar with little steel wheels at either end. "What is that?" she asked.

"A dumbbell. Somebody gave it to Joey. He wants to build his muscles and be a Tarzan suddenly," Mama said.

"He's enough of a dumbbell without it," Molly said.

"It's good he didn't hear you," Mama said.

"Where did he go in such a hurry?" Molly asked.

"I have no room in the house. I told him to ask Mr. Chiodo if he could keep the dumbbell in the Democratic club. Mr. Chiodo is the boss there." Mama glanced at the clock. "Turn it on, it's time," she said.

Molly did.

"We'll see now if Chichi kept the present Charles gave her, and if she went to Chicago with him," Mama said. She opened the oven door and looked inside at the cake. Then she sat down at the table.

As Molly took hold of the loose wire, the theme song rose up, and soon Papa David and Chichi, his adopted daughter, were talking about the job Chichi had been offered in Chicago. It was a good job, but Chichi didn't want to go to Chicago and leave the old man alone.

As Molly and Mama sat listening, Papa came home from work. No one was allowed to speak when Mama's programs were on. He looked at them, then made himself a glass of tea from the kettle that was always on the stove, and went into the living room to drink it.

Then Rebecca came home, carrying her sucking blanket. Molly noticed that her sister's mouth was red, and knew she had been eating spaghetti in Mrs. Chiodo's house again. Rebecca wasn't allowed to eat there. The food in Mrs. Chiodo's house wasn't kosher. Molly made a face at her sister.

"What happened?" Rebecca asked Mama, ignoring her.

"Shhh," Mama said. "Chichi gave back the present to Charles. And she's not going to Chicago."

"Ma, is Rebecca ever going to be old enough to stop carrying that rag around?"

"Shhh," Mama said, listening.

Rebecca climbed up on a chair and sat with them. Molly kept moving her hand around on the table, wondering why Rebecca, who noticed everything, had nothing to say about the ring.

"How do you like my ring?" Molly finally asked.

"Shhh," Mama said.

Rebecca glanced at the ring, then stuck the rag in her mouth and went back to listening.

Mama switched off the radio when the theme song came on again. "Oh," she said, "how I love that Chichi. What a wonderful girl. And Papa David, what a wonderful man. I wish they lived in this building, so I could have them as neighbors."

"What, you don't have enough wonderful neighbors without them?" Papa asked, coming in from the living room. "You have wonderful Mrs. Baumfeld upstairs, and wonderful Mrs. Bloom in back."

"Never mind with your cracks, Avram," Mama said.

Hearing Mrs. Bloom's name reminded Molly that she had homework. "What Nature Means to Me." There was some grass in the concrete backyard, where Molly sometimes played. She had to go through Mrs. Bloom's window to get there. The grass, and the two trees on the street, were all Molly knew of nature. But they meant nothing to her. She wondered how she was going to write the composition.

She looked around at her family. Mama was at the stove, checking on the pot of *gefilte fish* that was cooking there. Papa was sitting at the table, cracking walnuts and crumbling them into little pieces, for the cake. And Rebecca was playing with her little plastic doll with the dented belly.

Molly wondered if maybe they could help her.

"Ma, what does nature mean to you?" she asked.

"A good nature I like, a bad nature I don't," Mama said.

"Not that kind of nature, I mean trees and flowers," Molly said.

"Flowers I love," Mama said.

Molly turned to Papa. "Pa, what does nature mean to you?"

"On a nice day, I enjoy it," he said.

Rebecca piped up. "Mrs. Chiodo has flowers in the backyard," she said.

Molly was surprised. She hadn't been aware of that. A fence separated Mrs. Bloom's yard from Mrs. Chiodo's, and Molly had never been able to look through or over it.

"Well, what do flowers mean to you?" Molly asked, resenting her little sister for always coming up with some answer and admiring her at the same time.

"Mrs. Chiodo can't bring them in the house," Rebecca said. "They make Mr. Chiodo sneeze."

"The flowers?" Molly asked.

Rebecca looked away. She always said only what she wanted to and no more.

"Sure," Mama said as she washed her hands at the sink. "Some people get hay fever. Flowers make them sneeze." She removed the cake from the oven and set it on the windowsill to cool. "Why are you asking?"

"I have to write a composition for homework," Molly said. As she thought about it, she wondered whether she might feel something if she paid closer attention to nature.

"Ma, can I take a chair out in the backyard?" she asked.

"You have to ask Mrs. Bloom if you can go out," Mama said.

"I will."

"The chair is too heavy, you can't carry it."

"I'll carry it," Papa said.

"Avram, I don't want you carrying," Mama said. "You are not supposed to lift."

"It's only a chair."

"Never mind," Mama said.

Rebecca left the room and came back with her baby chair. It used to be Molly's, and she could still fit in it.

"Thanks," Molly said, wondering why she hadn't thought of it herself.

She saw her mother whisper to her father and knew they were talking about the baby. Mama was a good pretender, but Molly knew she was worried. Sadly, she took the chair and went down the hall.

Mrs. Bloom said she could use the window and even helped her out.

Molly set the chair down on the cement, beside the grass. She sat for a while daydreaming, looking at the ring and reminding herself of Bette Davis, except she couldn't turn the ring the way Bette Davis did—it was too tight for that.

After a while, she stared at the grass and tried hard to concentrate. *It's green*, she told herself. *Some of it is short, some long. The earth is brown.* She saw it all but felt nothing.

She tried smiling at the grass, hoping that would make her feel something. But it was no use.

She glanced up at the windows on the second floor. From Mrs. Marcus's house, she would be able to see all the yards. Then maybe she would feel something. But her mother didn't want her going up to Mrs. Marcus's. When her husband was out of town, an Irish policeman came to visit her, and Mama didn't like her for it.

Suddenly Molly got an idea. Sometimes, when she didn't know the answer to something, or couldn't understand a subject, she wrote a poem about that. Miss McCabe always accepted it. She seemed not to mind. And she usually gave her a good mark for it.

She thought and thought, and after a while she had this poem written in her head:

"What Nature Means to Me"

I do not care for flowers,
I do not care for trees,
You see, I have hay fever,
And nature makes me sneeze.

She grabbed up the little chair and quickly climbed back in through the window so she could write down the poem before she forgot it.

4

ROSH HASHANAH

Miss McCabe gave Molly a B+ for the poem and a B for the composition because it was too short. A lot of kids were still sick and the morning dragged on. Miss McCabe's nose was red and Molly wondered if the teacher was getting the grippe too.

After lunch there was spelling, and after that Miss McCabe told everyone to stay away from people with germs, and asked each person in the class to write a letter to an absent classmate. Everyone looked around the room to see who was missing, and began. Molly wrote Tsippi a letter telling her how much she missed her. She decided to leave it in Tsippi's mailbox on the way home.

"Class," Miss McCabe said, "the Jewish children have a holiday starting this evening, Rosh Hashanah. It's their New Year. They will not be back to school until Monday. Then ten days later, they have the end of this holiday, Yom Kippur."

Molly marveled that Miss McCabe knew so much. She wasn't even Jewish.

"Yippee!" one of the Jewish boys yelled and ran out the door.

"*Nyaa!* The Jews have all the luck," an Italian boy grumbled.

On her way home, Molly crossed the street and put the letter she had written into Tsippi's mailbox. Then, looking forward to the holiday and the arrival of company, she ran home to help her mother.

"It smells good in here," she cried as she opened the door.

Mama's voice answered from another room: "A *tsimmes* is cooking and a turkey's in the oven."

Molly knew Mama wanted the silverware polished, and she got busy polishing it. She liked seeing the tarnish disappear as she rubbed, and the silver show through. Mama kept leaving whatever she was doing to run to the stove and check on the cooking.

Molly sniffed. "Umm, what a smell. Delicious," she said, as Mama stood over the stove, removing the scum from the soup with a wooden spoon. "*Nu*, sure," she said. "On a holiday, when there are good things to eat, it smells good. Better than perfume."

Molly stepped back to admire the table. It all looked so nice, with the good dishes out and the good *Shabbos* silverware, and the candles and napkins and wine glasses. The kitchen table and the folding bridge table Mama had borrowed from Mrs. Baumfeld, for the children to sit at, had been shoved together and covered with a tablecloth, and it looked like one big table.

"Move, please," Mama said, carrying a pot to the stove. "Molly," she added, "put the honey on the table, with a dish underneath, so it doesn't drip."

Molly tried to remember what the honey stood for. "Ma, I forgot, why do we have honey again?" she asked, getting the jar from the cupboard and putting it on the table.

"For the New Year," Mama said. "We dip in *challa*,

sometimes apple, before we eat, to start off the new year with a sweet taste."

Rebecca came in from the next room, where Papa had taken her to help her get dressed for the holiday.

"I smell *tsimmes*," Rebecca said.

"You're right," Mama answered.

"Don't give me any raisins in the *tsimmes*."

"You don't have to eat them."

"I don't want them on my plate."

"All right, I'll pick them out for you," Mama said.

"Could I have a sour pickle instead?"

Mama glanced at her. "What instead? There is no instead. On this holiday we don't eat anything sour, only sweet things."

Molly looked her sister over. She was wearing a dress that Molly had outgrown. But her shoes were brand-new.

"You look nice, Rebecca," Molly said, giving her sister a hug.

"Don't," Rebecca said, shaking herself free. "You'll make my shoes dirty."

"How am I going to make your shoes dirty?"

"You might step on them."

Molly turned to Mama. "Did you hear that? Ma, you tell me to be nice to her. But look how she acts. What kind of person is she?"

Mama stood gazing at Rebecca as if she wondered the same thing. "Molly, count the dishes, see if there's a place for everyone," she said.

"I counted already."

"Count again, don't be gritty. We can afford it."

"*Greedy*, not gritty," Molly said.

". . . Ten, eleven," Molly said, pointing with the finger of her left hand, enjoying the sight of the ring.

"Something's wrong," Mama said. She closed one eye and counted aloud. "Six of us," she said. "Esther and Mordi and Selma is nine, and Bessie and Heshy. Eleven is right. So what's wrong?"

Papa came in all dressed up. "All we need is ten plates," he said. "The baby eats from the high chair."

"That's it," Mama said. She removed a plate and squeezed two chairs closer together, then shoved the high chair into the space.

"Molly, go change. The children's *shul* starts soon. Everyone is dressed."

"Joey's not," Molly said.

Mama looked at her. "What kind of answer is that? He's not here."

Molly laughed. "You said—everybody," she answered.

"The bathroom is free now," Papa said. "Go at least and wash up, before Joey comes home. I don't want banging on doors later."

"You don't look nice, Molly," Rebecca said. "You have to look nice for *shul*."

Molly stared at her sister. "Ma, did you hear that? What a nerve!" she said.

Rebecca turned to Papa. "Am I going to *shul* with you, or with Molly?"

"Not with me," Molly said. "I'm not taking you anyplace."

"You can go later, with the grown-ups," Papa said. "It doesn't matter which *shul* you go to. God hears us wherever we are, when we ask to be forgiven for our sins and to be blessed in the new year."

"What's a sin, Papa?" Rebecca asked.

"A sin is when you do something wrong, something to hurt another person."

"But I didn't do anything wrong, Papa," Rebecca said.

"Then you have nothing to worry about. God will bless you," Papa said.

Molly thought of all the times she had seen Rebecca leaving Mrs. Chiodo's house with red spaghetti sauce all over her mouth. Mrs. Chiodo wasn't kosher, and it was a sin to eat nonkosher food.

"Pa," Molly said, "is it a sin if a person eats spaghetti and meatballs?"

"Not in our house—our house is kosher," Papa said.

"What if the person eats it in Mrs. Chiodo's house?" Molly asked.

"If it's Mr. Chiodo, it's not a sin."

"No, I mean a Jewish person," Molly said.

"It's not kosher there, so it would be a sin."

"Mrs. Chiodo is a good friend, but nobody in our family eats there," Mama said. She turned to Molly. "How many times do I have to tell you? Get dressed. It's soon time to go to *shul*."

Molly looked at her sister and regretted her words. Rebecca's face had clouded over with worry. She left the room, dragging her duck along. Molly was sorry. She had only meant to tease her, not to frighten her. The seriousness of what she had done dawned on her. On Rosh Hashanah, when her actions were being judged in heaven, she had hurt another person; she had committed a sin.

She looked up, hoping God wouldn't punish her. She would have given anything to take Rebecca's fear away, to make her feel good again. She wondered what she could do to please her. Suddenly she had an idea.

The last time Selma-the-Communist had come, she had brought a *Saturday Evening Post* magazine. It had a picture in it of a little red-cheeked girl advertising soup. Rebecca was crazy about that little girl. Selma had had to tear the page out and give it to her. Molly decided to get Rebecca another picture of that little girl. But she needed fifteen cents for that.

The front door opened and Joey came in. From his red face, Molly could tell that he had been lifting weights at the Democratic club. He went to the icebox and got himself a soda.

Molly looked around, wondering whom to ask for money. Papa had picked up his prayer book and sat at the table reading it. Mama was washing out a pot. Molly decided to ask her.

"Ma," she said, "Gentiles give each other presents on New Year's. Why can't the Jews?"

"They give presents on Christmas, not New Year's," Joey said, and took a swig from the bottle of cream soda.

"Why?" Mama asked. "Who do you want to give a present?"

Molly raised a finger to her lips, to show it was a secret. "Remember the little girl in the magazine that Selma brought that time, that Rebecca was so crazy about?"

"So?" Mama said.

"I want to buy her a magazine. Can you lend me

fifteen cents? I'll pay you back. I get a penny a day allowance. I won't take my allowance for fifteen days."

Papa looked up. "Why do you want to buy her a present? It's not her birthday. It's not Chanukah."

"For Rosh Hashanah, for the New Year," Molly said.

Joey wiped his mouth on his sleeve. "Oh, boy," he said. "I bet she did something wrong. Now she's trying to do a good deed, to wipe the sin away."

Molly glared at her brother.

"There are no sinners in our family, only angels," Mama said. "Come on," she added, giving Joey a shove. "Get dressed. It's time to go to the children's *shul*."

Joey put his hand in his pocket. "Tell you what I'm gonna do," he said, imitating the man on the radio who talked like that. "I made twenty cents delivering groceries this week. I could always use a good deed." He held out a dime. "Here, take it, before I change my mind."

Molly was at a loss for words. Ten cents was a fortune. She looked gratefully at her brother and took it.

"Look at that," Papa said. "First Molly, then Joey, two good deeds in ten minutes."

"You see," Mama said. "I told you it was a house full of angels."

Papa took a nickel out of his pocket. "I could use a good deed myself," he said, giving it to Molly. "Now you have enough."

"For keeps? I don't have to pay it back?" Molly asked.

"For keeps," Papa said.

Molly couldn't get over her good fortune. She put her sweater on and ran across the street to the candy store. She was back in no time, with *The Saturday Evening Post* open to the page with the soup ad. She waved it at Mama and Papa as she went past them to the room she shared with Rebecca. Her sister was sitting on the floor, trying to balance the doll on the duck.

"Guess what I have for you," Molly said, holding the magazine behind her back.

Rebecca did not look up and did not answer.

"You'll like it," Molly said.

"I don't want to talk to you, you're a stool pigeon," Rebecca said.

The words stung Molly. "I didn't mean it, honest I didn't," she said. "Besides, I didn't say you ate Mrs. Chiodo's meatballs. I said, 'What if a person did?' Don't you remember? Maybe you didn't hear me. But that's what I said."

Rebecca glanced away as she thought back. "I never eat the meatballs. Only the spaghetti," she said.

"See?" Molly said. "Spaghetti is no sin. Spaghetti is kosher. Only the meatballs aren't kosher."

Rebecca looked up. "Then will God bless me?"

"Sure!" Molly said, glad to have Rebecca talking to her again.

Rebecca leaned over, trying to see behind Molly's back.

"Here," Molly said, handing her sister the magazine. "A Rosh Hashanah present for you."

"*Ooooo*," Rebecca said, taking the picture, staring.

Molly was overjoyed. She had made her sister happy. "I'll tell you what else," Molly said. "I'm taking you to *shul* with me."

Rebecca looked up, grinning happily. Molly was so

pleased, she didn't know what to do. She glanced at the ring. Rebecca would be thrilled to try it on. Molly went to pull it off but couldn't. It was too tight. Annoyed, she gave it another yank.

"Molly!" Mama called from the kitchen.

"All right, I'm going," Molly called back, and ran into the closet to get dressed.

Rebecca kept stopping to dust off her new shoes as she, Joey, and Molly walked to the synagogue together. Once there, Joey went to sit on the boys' side, and Molly and Rebecca sat together with the girls. Molly said hello to the girls she knew. The children kept bouncing in and out of their seats and shouting across the aisle until Mr. Persky, one of the Hebrew teachers, came in. He was in charge of the children's *shul*. He walked to the front of the room and faced them.

"*Shana tova*, happy New Year, children," he said.

"*Shana tova*," they answered.

"Turn to page forty-two in the prayer book," he said.

The monitors were passing out books and Molly took one and opened it to the page. Rebecca pulled at her arm until Molly moved closer, so Rebecca could look in the book too. Suddenly some latecomers came rushing in and Molly and Rebecca moved over to make room for them on the bench. It was Hanna Gittel and some other girl. Hanna Gittel smiled at Molly as she got in. Molly had never seen her so close before. She was pretty.

"We will start with the blowing of the *shofar*, the ram's horn," Mr. Persky said, "which opens the Rosh Hashanah holiday. Steven will come up to blow it."

The *shofar* was hard to blow, and everyone giggled as he got up from where he sat next to Joey and walked to the front.

Steven took the *shofar* from Mr. Persky and put it to his lips. He blew into it with all his might. His face got red but no sound came out. He tried again and a tiny note peeped out and instantly died away.

The children started laughing. Molly saw Joey holding his sides.

"Why are they laughing?" Rebecca asked.

"Because he can't blow it, it's too hard," Molly said.

Mr. Persky looked up. "No laughing!" he called.

Everyone grew silent as Steven tried again. This time, as he blew, short little high sounds came out, one after the other.

"Very good," Mr. Persky said.

Beaming, Steven took his seat.

"Michael will read the opening prayer," Mr. Persky said.

Michael went to the front of the room. He and Joey were both being prepared for their Bar Mitzvahs, and they knew how to read the prayers.

"*Boruch atoh Adonai*, Blessed art thou, O Lord, our God . . ." he began, reading slowly.

The girl sitting behind Molly leaned forward and tapped Hanna Gittel on the shoulder. "Did you ever find your ring?" the girl asked.

Molly's heart stood still.

"No," Hanna Gittel whispered back.

"What ring?" the girl beside her asked.

"I lost my ring the other day, when I was playing in the school yard."

Molly felt a thumping in her head. Her mind was a jumble. Only one thought was straight: of all people, Hanna Gittel. She started to hide her finger but she knew that was wrong. The ring wasn't hers. She had to give it back. She put her hands in her lap and tried to slip it off, but couldn't budge it. She thought a moment. She couldn't very well give it back while it was still on her finger. How would that look? Turn to Hanna Gittel and say, I found your ring, but I can't get it off my finger? No, that would make her look like a crook. She had no business wearing a ring that wasn't hers.

Tonight, she told herself, she would get the ring off, one way or another. Then, tomorrow in *shul*, she would go up to Hanna Gittel and say, Is this the ring you lost? I found it outside. Yes, that's what she would do. For now, she slipped her hand under her thigh and sat on it.

"Was it valuable?" Molly heard the girl ask.

"My father gave it to me," Hanna Gittel whispered.

Mr. Persky looked up over his glasses. "There's talking on the girls' side," he said. He gave a silent warning, then called Joey to the platform, and Joey went up and read a prayer. When he was finished, everyone stood up and read the prayers together. Then they sang "*Adon Olam*, Master of the Universe." Molly knew the words and sang along, but Rebecca hadn't started Hebrew school yet and she just looked down at her shoes.

When *shul* was over everyone got up. Molly took Rebecca's hand and walked to the door with her. Joey ran up to them outside. "Tell Mama I'll be home soon. I'm going over to Izzie's house for a minute," he said, and ran off with his friend.

As Molly turned to walk home her heart skipped a beat. Hanna Gittel was walking toward her. It was about the ring, Molly was sure of it. Luckily, her left hand was hidden, holding Rebecca's hand.

"Hi, Molly. Is this your sister?" Hanna Gittel asked. Molly nodded.

"Did I see you in front of the tailor's on Thirteenth Avenue?" Hanna Gittel asked.

"Maybe," Molly said, relieved. "My friend Julie lives upstairs."

"Does she have red hair?"

Molly knew Hanna Gittel was only trying to be friendly. But she couldn't take a chance. Any minute Hanna Gittel could see the ring. Molly nodded and turned to go. "We have to get home. Our cousins from Brownsville are coming for *Yontiff*."

"Good-bye," Hanna Gittel called after her.

Molly found she now had something new to worry about. She wondered if Rebecca had heard the conversation in the *shul*. Every time Molly looked at her, she saw her admiring her shoes, or dusting them off. Even so, she could have heard. Small as she was, she could put two and two together, and see a connection between Molly's found ring and Hanna Gittel's lost one. The thought that her sister was walking along thinking to herself that Molly was a crook was more than Molly could stand. She had to find out what Rebecca was thinking.

"That girl, Hanna Gittel . . ." she said.

"What girl?" Rebecca asked.

"The one I was just talking to."

"She talks funny," Rebecca said.

"She's a refugee. Her English is still not so good," Molly said. "She was born in Europe. She and her mother escaped from Hitler."

"He didn't kill them?" Rebecca asked.

Molly felt easier. If Rebecca had heard the conversation in the *shul*, she would have brought it up. She was like that. "They were lucky, they escaped," Molly said. "I bet you don't remember who's waiting for you at home," she said, to change the subject.

"Mordi?" Rebecca asked.

"I bet he's there," Molly said. "But I didn't mean him. I meant the little girl in the magazine."

Rebecca looked up at her with a grin. "Yeah," she said.

Molly was convinced Rebecca hadn't heard. She felt a surge of happiness. "Let's skip," she said, knowing how Rebecca enjoyed being treated like one of the big girls.

They came to a stop. "Start with the right foot," Molly said.

They began to skip together. It took a while before Molly could fall into step with Rebecca, but after a few skips she found the right rhythm and soon they were skipping along in a nice, easy way. Molly felt so good, she could have skipped to the moon.

"Home!" she called as they reached the steps of the stoop.

5

THE COUSINS COME

Everyone was in the kitchen, hugging and kissing, when Molly and Rebecca came in. Mama was kissing Mordi, Aunt Esther was kissing Papa, and Selma came up to Rebecca and stood shaking her hand.

What a jerk! Molly thought, watching Selma. High heels, lipstick, and her hair in an upsweep, like Joan Crawford, and shaking hands with a little girl. Molly saw Rebecca wipe her hand on her dress and go out the door.

"Molly, dolly!" Aunt Esther called. "Come here, let me give you a kiss."

Molly wondered why, if her aunt wanted so much to kiss her, she couldn't walk over. But she reminded herself of Mama's words and went toward her with a smile. Mama had told her always to be nice to Aunt Esther, because of the hard life she'd had, bringing up two children alone. Her husband had been killed in Palestine, where he had gone to help the Jewish settlers fight Arabs who were attacking them. The Arabs had shot him.

As Molly dutifully presented herself for a kiss, she gave Selma the once-over. No one called her Selma-the-Communist to her face. Molly supposed she liked her cousin. Selma was pretty, and smart too. She was only sixteen, and going into Brooklyn College. But the Communist part, that's what Molly didn't like. Selma was always talking about how wonderful Russia was. And she was always arguing. She had only just arrived, and already she was arguing with Papa.

"Hi, Selma," Molly said. She kept a distance, in case Selma wanted to shake her hand too. Selma glanced up, waved, and turned back to Papa again.

"Why did you bring that paper in my house?" Papa asked, his voice rising.

Selma rolled up *The Daily Worker*, the Communist paper Papa had been talking about. "I have to have something to read on the subway," she said.

"Why didn't you leave it outside? You didn't have to bring it here."

Aunt Esther turned to Mama. "I told her to leave it," she said, sounding worried.

"But I'm not finished reading it," Selma said.

"Avram! Selma!" Mama said, hoping to silence them.

"You're not being democratic, Uncle," Selma said. "Besides, I could understand why you were against Russia when they were on Hitler's side of the war. But now they're fighting on the Allied side, with England against Germany."

Everyone was standing, watching them.

"That paper," Papa said, glaring at Selma, "and the whole subject, is not welcome in this house. In no Jewish home! Russia is against God, and against Jews."

Mama looked from Selma to Papa. "Please," she said. "It's Rosh Hashanah, the birthday of creation, the beginning of the new year. No politics today!"

"Laya's right," Aunt Esther said.

There are always arguments when she's around, Molly thought. She looked at Mordi, her little cousin. "Hi,

Mordi," she said, taking him in her arms and giving him a hug.

"How are you, Mordi?" she asked in the voice she used when she played make-believe with her friends.

"F-f-fine," Mordi answered.

Esther pointed to a bag she had placed on a chair. "Laya, put it in the icebox," she said.

Mama looked at her. "You made stuffed cabbage?"

"Fricassee, too," Esther said with a grin, knowing how much Mama liked it.

Mama clapped her hands together. "Wonderful!" she said, and put the things away.

"Ummmm," Selma said. "Everything smells delicious."

"Wait till you taste it," Mama said. She took Esther by the arm. "Let's go in the living room," she said. "When Bessie and Heshy come, we'll sit down to eat."

Molly saw Mama pull Papa aside. "Avram," Mama said. "Don't talk politics with Selma. The arguments upset Esther. They upset me too."

Esther turned to go into the living room. "Yaaki, sweetheart!" she cried, heading for the baby's crib. Mama and Papa followed her in.

Selma pulled a chair away from the table and sat down. "Where's Rebecca?" she asked.

"Somewhere," Molly said.

"And Joey?"

"He went to his friend's house for a minute. He'll be right back."

Molly fidgeted. She always felt like she was taking a test when Selma was around. That was another thing she didn't like about her cousin.

Selma nodded at the little room off the kitchen, where Joey slept. "Does the boarder still live here?"

Molly shook her head. "She moved away when Papa started working full time. We didn't need the money anymore."

"War is good for that. It makes jobs," Selma said.

Molly didn't know what her cousin was talking about. "America is not in the war," she said. She saw Rebecca come in from outside and go into the bathroom.

"No, but England is. And England needs clothes and guns and ammunition for its soldiers. And American factories make those things. War makes work for people. We can thank Hitler for making jobs in America."

Molly bristled, hearing the hated name of Hitler spoken of in that way. Hitler was killing Jews in Europe. And here was her cousin, saying Hitler made jobs.

"What's so good about Hitler?" Molly asked, indignant.

"I didn't say he was good. I said the war was good for making jobs," Selma said.

Molly couldn't let the subject go. "Hitler is killing Jews," she said, "and nobody lifts a finger to help," she added, borrowing a phrase she had heard Papa use.

Rebecca came into the kitchen. Molly could see from the red sauce all over her mouth that she had been at Mrs. Chiodo's house.

"Where were you?" Molly asked, knowing full well where she had been.

"I went to show Mrs. Chiodo my new shoes," Rebecca said.

Selma looked down. "They are very pretty," she said.

"They're new," Rebecca said.

"I can see that," Selma said.

Molly wet a paper napkin at the sink and wiped Rebecca's mouth.

"Stop!" Rebecca said.

"Do you want Mama to see the red?" Molly whispered.

Rebecca looked away. She turned to Selma. "I want to show you something," she said.

She went inside and came back with the magazine and showed the picture of the little girl.

"I remember that," Selma said. "It can't be the same one I gave you the last time I was here. That was months ago."

"Molly gave me this," Rebecca said.

Molly was worried about the ring. She kept pushing the thought to the back of her mind. Rebecca's words helped to make her feel good. She pulled out a chair and sat down. Then she tried to lift Mordi, but he was too heavy. "Come, sit with me," she said, moving over and making room for him on the chair.

"What are you going to be when you grow up?" Selma asked Molly.

"I don't know," Molly said. "Mama says a journalist. Papa says I'd make a good president."

"Of what?" Selma asked with a laugh.

Molly shrugged. "I don't know," she said, realizing she had never bothered to find out.

"I'm going to b-b-be a f-f-flyer, l-like Lindbergh," Mordi said.

"How come?" Molly asked.

"You don't have to t-t-talk," Mordi said. "You j-j-just fly the plane."

Selma laughed. "That's a good choice," she said.

"I'm going to be a leckrishan," Rebecca said.

"An electrician?" Selma repeated. "That's a funny job for a girl."

"Yesterday she said she was going to be an iceman," Molly said. "It changes every day."

Selma glanced at Molly's hand. "That's a nice ring. Did you get it in the five-and-ten?"

"No," Molly said, and put her hand behind her back. She did not want to talk about the ring. She was glad to look up and see the door open and Joey come walking in. "Hi, Selma," he said, going over and giving her a kiss.

"Joey! You've grown since the last time I saw you," Selma said.

"I didn't get taller," Joey said. "But I started to lift weights. It makes me look bigger."

"What are you trying to do, become one of those muscle builders, with the bulging muscles?" Selma asked.

"Nah," Joey said. "I just want to build myself up so the big guys won't pick on me." He sat down on the windowsill. "I have a job too," he added proudly. "I deliver groceries after school."

"Hitler made your job," Rebecca said.

Selma laughed. "Where did you hear that?" she said. "You weren't even in the room when we were talking about Hitler."

"Don't worry about her," Molly said. "She hears everything. Even a block away." As she said it, she

wondered again if Rebecca had heard the conversation in the *shul*.

"I hear B-B-Bessie's voice in the hall," Mordi said.

A moment later, the door opened and Bessie and Heshy came in carrying bags and boxes. Bessie put a white bakery box on the table.

"*Taitlach!*" Joey yelled.

"Right," Bessie said with a grin, her gold tooth showing.

Mama, Papa, and Esther came rushing in from the living room, and again everyone was going from one to the other, hugging and kissing.

"I love *taitlach*," Rebecca said.

"M-m-me, too," Mordi said. "B-but it gets s-s-stuck in my teeth."

Molly also liked the sticky honey-and-nuts pastry, but she said nothing. She was trying not to be noticed by Heshy. She didn't like him. He smelled of cigars. She regretted that Aunt Bessie had ever married him. She hardly saw her aunt anymore. She stayed in Coney Island, where Heshy worked as a waiter on the boardwalk, because he thought the sea air was so good there. Molly backed away from the group, hoping he would think he had already kissed her.

"Molly!" he cried. "I kissed everybody except you."

Molly looked down as he bent over, and his kiss landed on her head. "The cigar," she said, feeling she ought to say something.

He showed her the cigar in his hand. "I'm only holding it, it's not lit."

Molly didn't want to be rude to him. She forced a little smile on her face. "Oh," she said.

"Let's sit, people," Mama said. "Everybody's here. Children, the bridge table is for you."

Everyone took seats. Selma sat at the grown-up table. Molly sat next to Joey, at the children's table. Papa put on his skullcap, and gave Heshy and Joey skullcaps too. Mama asked Esther to take the chopped liver and chopped egg appetizers out of the icebox, and went to bring the baby in. She put him in the high chair, but he was cranky and started to cry and she had to put him back in the crib again.

Papa said the blessing over the *challa* bread, then sliced it and gave everyone a piece to dip in the honey.

"I don't like the way the baby looks," Mama said almost to herself as she took her seat.

"He'll be fine. Don't worry," Papa said. He made a blessing over the honey, dipped in his piece of bread, and passed the jar along.

"Come on, everyone," Papa said. "Dip the *challa* in the honey and eat it, to start off the new year sweetly."

"Aunt Laya," Selma said, "do you have an apple? I'd rather dip that. It's less fattening."

"Gladly," Mama said, putting some chopped liver on Rebecca's plate. She got up.

Molly glared at her cousin. What a nerve! How did she know they had apples in the house? How did she know they could afford to let her have one? Why couldn't she have taken a tiny piece of *challa*, and not made a fuss?

Mama handed Selma an apple, and a knife to peel it with. "Thanks for asking. You gave me a chance to do a good deed," Mama said with a laugh.

"That's right," Papa said. "The more good deeds we do, the more sins we wash away."

Molly winced. She could see Hanna Gittel's face before her eyes. She reached down and felt the ring. But she had committed no sin. The minute she got it off she was going to give the ring back.

"Thank God, I have no sins," Heshy said.

"Who said so?" Aunt Bessie asked. "What about the mosquito you killed in the country, in the summer?" She laughed, showing her gold tooth.

Molly took the jar of honey as it came her way. She dipped her piece of *challa* into it, scooping up an extra amount of honey, hoping it would help sweeten the year for her.

"What if we have more bad deeds than good deeds?" she asked, hurrying to eat the bread before the honey dropped on the tablecloth.

"We pray for forgiveness. We do that always," Papa said. "But this holiday is different. We pray not only for ourselves, but for others as well."

Molly remembered Selma's words and thought she would get back at her. "Hitler, too?" she asked, intending to be funny.

Papa stared at her. "No, not Hitler."

"What's the matter with you, Molly?" Mama asked.

Molly could feel everyone's eyes on her. "I was only trying to make a joke," she said.

"That's no joke," Papa said.

"Molly, I'll give you the chance to do a good deed," Joey said. "Pass me the chopped egg, please."

Grateful to her brother for changing the subject, Molly passed him the plate.

Mama finished eating, then took her empty plate and

put it in the sink. She went to the sideboard, removed the paper covering from the turkey, and brought it to the table.

"*Nu?*" she said. "How do you like this bird?"

"A beauty," Esther said.

"It looks great," Selma said.

"Fit for a king," Heshy said.

"Made especially for you, King Heshy," Mama said. Bessie laughed.

"And the *tsimmes*, just smell that!" Selma said, as Mama brought the serving dish to the table.

"I bet they have nothing like that to eat in Russia," Papa said.

"Avram!" Mama cried, warning him not to say anything that would start an argument.

Papa straightened his skullcap and Molly listened to him say the blessing: "Blessed art thou, O Lord, our God, King of the Universe, who has kept us in life, and preserved us, and enabled us to reach this season."

"Amen," everyone answered.

"And may it please God, let our little Yaaki be well, and grant him health in the new year," Papa said.

"Amen," everyone repeated.

Papa picked up the knife and started to carve. "Joey," he said, "I think I remember you told me before you were fasting, so I'm not going to give you anything."

"Wait a minute!" Joey said. "You fast on Yom Kippur, not now. Anyhow, I never said that."

Everyone laughed.

"Give him the thigh, he likes it," Mama said.

"I want the wing," Molly said. She thought of the ring and felt sick.

"I want the neck," Rebecca said.

"What do you want, Mordi?" Papa asked.

"I w-w-want the p-p-part that sings," Mordi said with a smile.

Papa looked at him. "What part sings?"

"I d-d-don't know," Mordi said.

Everyone laughed, all but Molly.

"Here, take the part that walks," Papa said, and gave him a leg.

"I don't want the raisins," Molly heard Rebecca say.

"I'll take them," Joey said.

Molly watched as he picked raisins from Rebecca's plate. She thought of him on the stage, in the children's *shul*, reading the prayer. It reminded her of Hanna Gittel— and tomorrow.

"What time is *shul* in the morning, Joey?" she asked.

"There is no children's *shul* tomorrow, didn't you hear the teacher tell you?"

Molly sat up. She had forgotten!

"Mr. Persky's going to his own *shul* tomorrow," Joey added, explaining. "The Hebrew school is closed till Yom Kippur.

"That's right," Papa said. "Whoever wants can come to Temple Emanuel with me tomorrow."

"I'll go," Rebecca said.

"I won't be going; I have to see a friend of mine," Selma said.

Molly felt relieved. As she thought about it, it occurred to her that she might never have to give the ring back. Yom Kippur was ten days away. That was a long time. Anything could happen. Hanna Gittel could move away. Molly might never see her again.

As Esther and Bessie cleared the table, Mama filled everyone's glass with tea and passed around little glass cups with stewed fruit for dessert. Papa said a blessing to himself and ate some.

"Where's the *taitlach*?" Joey asked.

"Coming, coming," Mama said, hurrying to put the loaf on a plate and bring it to the table.

"I love it," Rebecca said.

"M-m-me too," Mordi said.

Joey pinched off the top layer and was about to put it in his mouth, but Papa pushed his hand away.

"Say the blessing first," Papa said.

Papa sipped his tea through a piece of sugar in his mouth. "Come on, everybody, let's sing," he said, starting a song they all knew.

Everyone joined in.

Molly felt good; her voice rose and rose until she was singing at the top of her lungs.

Rebecca stuck her fingers in her ears.

"Molly, you'll wake the baby," Mama said.

"Not so loud," Papa said. "It's a kitchen, not a stadium."

Molly broke off a piece of the *taitlach* loaf, put it into her mouth, and, enjoying the sweet taste of honey and nuts, sang along more quietly.

6

PUNISHMENT

In the morning, Molly sat in the living room with her
library book open on her lap. Papa, Rebecca, Aunt Esther,
and Mordi had gone to *shul*. Molly had decided not to go
with them. Rosh Hashanah wasn't as important as Yom
Kippur. Papa didn't force her to go when she said she
wanted to stay home and read. She had volunteered to sit
with the baby, if Mama wanted to go too, but Mama said
Yaaki wasn't feeling well, and she wanted to stay close to
him.

Molly stopped reading and looked around, enjoying
the emptiness of the apartment. Only she and Yaaki were
in the living room. And it was nice to have the couch all to
herself. Bessie and Heshy had left last night, after supper.
But the house was still crowded, with Esther and Selma
and Mordi there. Molly was happy when company came.
And she loved Aunt Esther and Mordi and maybe even
Selma. But she would be glad when they left on Sunday.

Mama came in, lifted the baby out of the crib, and put
him on the couch to dress him.

"I'll take him out for some air. It'll do him good," she
said.

Molly looked at the baby beside her. She could see he
didn't feel well. She bent to kiss his foot and he made a little
movement with his lips, as if he wanted to smile.

"Come, Yaaki," Mama said. "We'll go outside and

you'll get rosy cheeks." She sat him up and buttoned his sweater. Then she put his little blue hat on his head and placed him in the carriage.

"Yaaki's going bye-bye," Molly said, smiling at the baby.

"It's a nice day—why are you sitting inside?" Mama asked.

"I like to sit on the couch alone and read," Molly said.

Mama put her sweater on and left pushing the carriage.

Molly liked having the couch to herself, but she couldn't read. She found herself thinking about Hanna Gittel. She hoped the girl was moving. Or that she was going away for a long time. But maybe she wasn't. Maybe she lived right around the corner. Or on the next block. Molly could run into her any minute. She should try and find out about her. But who knew her? Julie! Hanna Gittel had mentioned Julie. Maybe Julie knew something. Molly decided to go see her friend.

She put on an old blue sweater of Mama's that had a pocket, in case she had to hide her hand, and went out.

Mama was rolling the carriage up and back in front of the stoop, talking to a neighbor lady.

"Ma, I'm going to Julie's house," Molly said.

Mama nodded. "Why are you wearing that sweater?" she asked.

"I like it."

"You're swimming in it. Why don't you wear your sweater?"

"I like this one," Molly said, going down the street.

The neighborhood seemed deserted. Molly knew that

Thirteenth Avenue was empty because everyone was in *shul*. Only the Italian bakery and the dairy restaurant were open.

Molly opened the door of Julie's building and went up the stairs. She knocked and went in. She found Julie ironing, the laundry bag open on the chair next to her. Molly could see from the pile of folded handkerchiefs and pillowcases that she was ironing the flat, easy things.

"Hi," Julie said, blowing the hair out of her eyes.

"Hi," Molly answered. Molly glanced around. Julie's house wasn't all cleaned up and straightened for the holiday. Molly felt sorry for her. "Isn't your mother home?" she asked, suspecting that Mrs. Roth was stretched out on the couch in the other room.

"She's resting," Julie said, nodding toward the living room.

"Who is it, Julie?" Mrs. Roth's voice called.

"Molly."

Molly leaned against the kitchen wall. "Julie," she said, "there's a girl in my Hebrew class who knows you. Hanna Gittel is her name."

"Hanna Gittel?" Julie repeated, stumbling over the name. "I can't even say it."

"It's a Jewish name, from Europe," Molly said. "Do you know her?"

"Does she have short blond hair?" Julie asked, taking a pillowcase from the laundry bag.

"No, wavy brown hair."

"Is she tall?"

Molly laughed. "She's smaller than me and skinnier than you."

"I guess I don't know her," Julie said. "How come she knows me?"

Molly shrugged. "I don't know."

"Julie!" Mrs. Roth called from inside. "I don't want you going out. We have to get ready."

"I'm not," Julie called back. She smiled at Molly. "Guess what," she said. "Mrs. Rubel, the lady upstairs, invited me and my mother to dinner when her husband comes home from *shul*."

Molly was glad Julie had someplace to go. *Maybe she'll get something better to eat than hot dogs*, she thought.

"I feel so lucky," Julie said, running the iron over the pillowcase. "We're both lucky, Molly. Look, Tsippi's sick, the two Naomis are sick, and you and me, we're okay."

"I didn't know the Naomis were sick too," Molly said.

"Ohhhh," Mrs. Roth moaned in the next room.

Molly flinched. The sound always surprised her. It gave her the heebie-jeebies. She went to the door. "See you later," she said, and left.

Molly was disappointed. She had hoped Julie was going to tell her that Hanna Gittel was moving away, or something. But Julie didn't even know her. Molly kept glancing at the ring as she walked home. She wondered if Hanna Gittel's mother had hit her for losing the ring. Or yelled at her. A picture of Hanna Gittel crying came to her.

Mama was in the kitchen, getting lunch ready. Yaaki was asleep in the crib. Molly stood over him, looking at him. That wheezing sound came from his chest and it frightened her.

"Ma," she said, going into the kitchen, "Yaaki made that sound again."

"I know. He's not feeling well," Mama said sadly.

Molly sat watching Mama for a while, then she got up and set the table. Soon everyone was back from *shul*. Papa and Joey went to the sink to wash their hands and say the hand-washing prayer.

"Selma's not back yet?" Aunt Esther asked.

"Not yet," Mama said.

"I hope we d-d-don't have to wait for her t-t-to eat," Mordi said. "I'm s-s-starving."

"Absolutely not," Esther said. "The friend is a Communist too. They could talk about Russia for a week."

Rebecca walked up to Molly. "Guess who I saw in *shul*."

"Who?" Molly asked.

"The refugee girl," Rebecca said. "The one who lost her ring."

Molly felt the room spin. She waited for her sister to say more. But Rebecca said nothing. She went into her room and came out with the magazine, holding the picture of the little girl close to her chest. By some miracle, Molly thought, Rebecca had made no connection between Hanna Gittel's lost ring and Molly's.

"Did you talk to her?" Molly asked after a moment.

"I saw her but she didn't see me," Rebecca said.

"Sit down, everybody," Mama said. "Children, wash the hands first, please."

Molly washed, then sat down at the table, where everyone else was already seated. Just as Mama brought the pot of soup to the table, the door opened and Selma came in. She looked into the pot and smacked her lips.

"Perfect timing," she said and sat down.

Everyone was eating and talking, but Molly couldn't hear a word. She should have told Hanna Gittel right away about the ring, even though it was stuck. At least she would have known that her ring wasn't lost. Again a picture of Hanna Gittel crying came to Molly's mind.

"Molly, you're not eating," she heard Mama say.

"Yes, I am," she said, and took a mouthful of *tsimmes* to prove it.

"How come you're so quiet?" Selma asked.

"I'm not," Molly said, wishing her cousin would stick to Russia and mind her own business.

As everyone talked around the table, Molly thought about Hanna Gittel. She wished she knew where Hanna Gittel lived. She saw a picture of herself, rushing over to Hanna's Gittel's house and showing her the ring, and of Hanna Gittel drying her eyes because now she knew the ring wasn't lost. Reality broke in on Molly's thoughts. Now she knew for sure Hanna Gittel hadn't moved. That meant she would be seeing her in *shul*, on Yom Kippur. Molly looked down at the ring, hating it.

That night, in bed, she tried to get the ring off and couldn't. A panic seized her. What if she never got it off? What if it was stuck forever?

Despite the presence of the cousins, despite the set table and the good food, Molly had little sense of holiday. Rosh Hashanah came and went without her noticing. Her thoughts were on the ring, and she kept pulling at it.

On Sunday her finger hurt so from being pulled, she kept going into the bathroom to run cold water over it. Selma kept asking what she was doing in there so much.

Molly thought her cousin should mind her own business. She either pretended not to hear or answered, "Nothing."

At last, after lunch, the cousins left. Molly was glad to see them go this time. She watched them through the window. It seemed cold and gray outside, like her mood. Joey and Rebecca went out to play anyhow. But she was too miserable to move. For a while, she sat quietly in the living room—Yaaki was asleep—pretending to be busy with schoolwork. Every so often she went into the bathroom to run cold water over her finger. Then, so her parents wouldn't get suspicious, she sat down at the kitchen table with Papa and watched Mama prepare corn soup for supper. When they weren't looking, she blew on her finger.

Before long, Rebecca and Joey were home and everyone sat down to eat. A moment later, Molly's misery shifted. Her finger no longer mattered. Yaaki had let out a terrible cry and everyone jumped up and ran to the living room. Papa lifted Yaaki out of the crib and held him, patting his back. Then Mama did. The children stood watching, frightened and helpless. Molly couldn't stand to see the baby cry. His face was red. His eyes were shut tight and two tiny white teeth showed in the open mouth. Gradually, his cries stopped. He seemed to fall asleep. Mama put him back in the crib.

"Supper is on the table, let's finish eating," Mama said.

Slowly everyone returned to the kitchen. Joey broke bits of bread into his soup and ate silently. Mama put Rebecca in her lap and fed her. Molly could not eat. She sat listening to the silence, afraid to speak.

After supper, Papa brought the radio in from the

living room. "It's Sunday, the good programs are on," he said, putting the radio on the table and plugging it in. He sat down, turned it on, and held the wire in back. Soon Baby Snooks's voice came up. Molly usually liked listening to her. But she couldn't tonight. She had heard a wheezing sound and kept getting up and going into the living room to look into the crib.

"Come, Rebecca," Mama said when she had finished eating.

Rebecca collected her sucking rag, the duck, and her doll, and followed Mama into the bedroom. Soon Eddie Cantor came on. Joey said he had homework to do and went to his room. Molly remained sitting. She thought it was better to stay in the lighted kitchen with Papa, amid sound. After a few minutes Mama came back into the kitchen and put the dishes away. Molly didn't know if Papa was listening to Eddie Cantor, but he sat quietly, drumming his fingertips on the table.

Suddenly Molly did not want to sit in the lighted kitchen after all. She wanted to be alone, in the darkness, where no one could see her. She said good night and went to wash up. She glanced into the crib as she went into her room and pressed her lips together in a kiss. Rebecca was fast asleep when she got into bed.

Molly's thoughts churned and churned. She could hear Papa open the bed in the living room, could hear Mama turn out the light, could hear them get into bed. The house was quiet, but there was no peace in it. Molly kept thinking the baby had stopped breathing. Once, it was so vivid she jumped out of the bed and ran to look. Mama and Papa woke up and found her hanging over the crib. She didn't want them to know she was worried, so she said she was going to the kitchen for a drink. It was a dumb excuse, she knew that. She didn't have to go anywhere near the crib to get to the kitchen. But she couldn't think of anything else to say.

She lay stiffly under the blanket and listened to the silence.

Suddenly the baby's loud cries filled the house. Molly leaped out of bed. Everyone was up and in the living room, standing around Papa. He had lifted the baby out of the crib and stood patting him. Mama stood watching, her hand covering her mouth.

"It's no use like this," Papa said. "I'll call the doctor." He handed Mama the baby. "It's too late to wake up Mrs. Baumfeld. I'll go to the drugstore."

Molly noticed when she glanced at Rebecca that her little sister's chin was trembling. She took her hand. Papa dressed and went out. While he was gone, Molly and Joey and Rebecca took turns making little baby noises at Yaaki, trying to get him to smile. Sometimes he did. Mostly his eyes were closed. His blond curls lay flat against his head with perspiration.

Terrible thoughts kept forming in Molly's mind. "Please, God," she said to herself, "don't let the baby die. Please God, I'm going to give back the ring—Hanna Gittel will have her ring back, only make the baby better." So no one would know how she felt, she reached out to *kootsie-koo* the baby and fondle his foot.

In a few minutes, Papa was back.

"The doctor said we should take him to the hospital," Papa said.

The word filled Molly with terror. Mama gasped. Rebecca started to cry. "Poor baby," Joey said.

"It's only common sense," Papa said, making his voice cheerful. "That's what a hospital is for, to make sick people better. We don't know what to do. They know how to take care of him. They'll make him better. . . ."

No one spoke. Molly's eyes filled with tears. She thought of Julie's words. True, she hadn't gotten the grippe, and that was lucky. But something much worse had happened. Her baby brother was being taken to the hospital. Nothing could be worse than that.

"What's the matter with everyone?" Papa asked. "I just told you, they'll make him better in the hospital. He'll be able to breathe again. Don't you want him to get better?"

Molly could not stop crying.

"There's nothing to worry about," Joey said weakly.

"I'll get ready," Mama said.

Papa put his hand on Molly's shoulder as he led her and Rebecca into the kitchen. "Do you want your brother to get better?" he asked.

"What do you think?" Molly said through her tears.

"Then stop crying. A baby can feel things. He'll feel that you're worried. It'll scare him."

"Me too?" Rebecca asked, tears streaming down her face.

"You too," Papa said.

Molly tried to blink her tears away, for the baby's sake. She wondered suddenly if Papa was going to the hospital too. She hoped not. She didn't want to be left with only Joey.

Mama came in carrying the baby. Molly looked away. It broke her heart to see Yaaki all dressed up in a sweater and his little blue hat, as if he were going someplace nice.

"Children," Mama said, "go back to bed." She spoke to Papa in Yiddish, which Molly didn't understand.

"Joey," Papa said, "get dressed and go with Mama."

"Me?" Joey asked. "I'm only a kid. What can I do in a hospital?"

"You'll do whatever Mama tells you," Papa said. "I'll stay here with Molly and Rebecca."

Rebecca started to bawl. "Don't go away, Papa," she cried.

"You stay, Pa," Molly added, in case Joey put up a fight against going.

"*Shah, shah*, children," Papa said. "I just told you I'm not going, didn't I?"

Joey went to his room to get dressed.

"Children," Mama said to Molly and Rebecca, "go back to bed, please. Molly, you have to go to school in the morning."

Molly looked up. How could she think of going to school, with the baby in the hospital? "I'll be too tired to go to school," she said.

"So, you'll be tired, big dill!" Mama said.

"*Deal*, not dill," said Molly, playing along.

"That's what I said, *dill*," Mama repeated.

The baby began to cry, and Mama rocked him in her arms.

Joey appeared, dressed for the street.

"Let's go," Mama said. She turned to Molly and

Rebecca. "Go to sleep, children," she repeated. "Don't wait for me to come home. It could take a long time."

Papa gave Molly and Rebecca each a hand. "Go ahead, Laya," he said. "We'll be all right."

The sight of Mama and Joey leaving with the baby almost broke Molly's heart. Her chin began to tremble. But remembering Papa's words, she bit back her tears.

"Come, children," Papa said, going with them into the bedroom. "I'll tell you a story. I know you're too big for stories, Molly," he added, "but if you don't like it, you don't have to listen."

Another time, Molly would have resented Papa's suggestion. Tonight she welcomed the thought of a story, of being able to close her eyes and just listen.

As the girls got into bed, Papa returned to the kitchen for a chair. Molly heard a knock on the front door, then she heard voices in the kitchen. A moment later, she was surprised to see Papa bring Mrs. Chiodo in.

Mrs. Chiodo handed Rebecca the sucking rag and sat down beside her. "Sweetheart," she said, taking Rebecca in her arms. Rebecca snuggled up to her. "I heard voices inna street. I look outta the window and see you mama. . . ."

Molly looked away. She wished someone were holding her.

"Papa—is—going to tell us—a—story," Rebecca said through her tears.

"Good," Mrs. Chiodo said.

"What kind of story would you like to hear?" Papa said.

"A story with a lamb in it," Rebecca said.

"Do you know that story? Did I ever tell it to you before?" Papa asked.

"No, but that's what I want to hear," Rebecca said. "Mrs. Chiodo wants to hear it too."

"Sure," Mrs. Chiodo said.

"All right," Papa began. "Once there was a little boy who had a little sheep."

"What color was it?" Rebecca asked.

"White."

"I want it to be a black sheep," Rebecca said.

"Fine, let it be a black sheep."

"I want the story to be about a little girl," Rebecca said.

Papa tried again. "Once there was a little girl who had a black sheep."

"I don't want her name to be Bo-Peep," Rebecca said.

"What shall it be?"

"Rebecca."

Molly stopped listening. Papa kept trying to make up a story, Rebecca kept changing it, and Mrs. Chiodo kept saying, "Attsa nice story." Molly closed her eyes, pretending to be asleep. She wished she had a real story to listen to. Then she wouldn't have to think. As it was, ugly thoughts troubled her mind. *What if the baby doesn't get better? What if he never comes back?* She took the ring between her fingers and pulled and pulled at it until her finger hurt.

When she opened her eyes, she saw Mrs. Chiodo tiptoeing out of the room. She glanced around. Rebecca was fast asleep. Papa was dozing in the chair.

A few minutes later she heard the front door open.

"Mama," she yelled, jumping out of bed and running into the kitchen. Papa and Rebecca were behind her. The three of them stood staring at the sight of Mama holding a sweater and little hat but no baby.

"*Nu*," Mama said, "the baby's in the hospital."

That word again. Molly shivered. She was afraid to, but she made herself ask. "Ma, what kind of place is it? What did they do to Yaaki?"

"He's in a room with other children," Mama said. "It's nice and clean. There are nurses and doctors. They take care of the children, good care. . . ." She looked at Papa. "I'll go see him in the morning."

Joey went to the icebox and took out an apple.

Rebecca started to bawl suddenly.

"Rebecca, darling, what is it?" Mama cried, running toward her.

Rebecca could hardly speak. "No-body picks me— u-up," she sobbed.

Mama lifted her in her arms and rocked her.

"I'm still—a—baby," Rebecca said through her tears.

"Of course you are," Mama said, swaying with her, kissing her hair, rocking her. "You are Mama's precious baby, my darling, my whole life."

"Mine too," Papa said, putting his arms around them.

Molly looked away. She wished somebody's arms could be around her. But she realized it served her right. She was only getting what she deserved.

"The doctor said Yaaki is going to be fine," Joey said.

Molly looked at her brother. Maybe Selma was right. He did seem bigger.

"Boy, am I tired," he said. "I'm going to sleep." He

took a last bite, tossed the core into the garbage, and went into his room.

Mama carried Rebecca into the living room and put her down on the bed. "Rebecca will sleep with me and Papa tonight," she said, "so we won't feel lonely."

Rebecca and her sucking rag both disappeared under the blanket.

"Molly," Mama said, "you'll have the whole bed to yourself for a change."

Molly tried to smile. Often she did wish she could have the whole bed to herself. But not tonight. She went back into her room. The bed seemed huge without Rebecca. As she got into it, she glanced over at the dent in the mattress where Rebecca slept and began to cry softly to herself.

She lay there listening to her parents talking in the next room. Their voices seemed far away. She felt suddenly as if she were growing smaller by the minute. Alarmed, she felt around the bed to see if she was still there. She was.

The frightening thoughts came back to plague her. She saw Yaaki, crying in a dark hospital, with strangers around him. She saw Hanna Gittel crying. Poor Hanna Gittel. First she had Hitler, then Molly. The thought saddened Molly, and she started crying all over again. "Crook!" she yelled under her breath. *Liar! On account of you, the baby is in the hospital. On account of your sin, the whole family is being punished. And Hanna Gittel, a poor refugee girl, is crying. Dirty, rotten, lousy, stinking crook!* she thought, pulling at the ring, yanking at it with all her might to punish herself and make her finger hurt.

She turned on her side and stared at the dent in the mattress. It made her feel so alone. Before she knew it, she was crying. She was worried. And afraid. But there was another feeling mixed in.

It was love. Her brother was precious and dear. She couldn't stand to see him hurting. She loved him. She loved Mama and Papa, too. And Rebecca and Joey. And Aunt Bessie—before she married Heshy. And Tsippi. Even Selma, her first best friend, from the old neighborhood.

The tears were coming hard and fast and the pillow was wet. Molly turned it over and snuggled up to the dent with it.

"I love you, Yaaki," she said, sobbing into the pillow. "I love you. . . ." She was about to go through all the names but decided there were too many. "I love you—ev-er-y-bo-dy," she said instead, letting the tears come.

7

THE HARDWARE STORE

The house seemed different to Molly in the morning. It wasn't only that the crib was empty. Everyone spoke in a sort of whisper and tiptoed around. It was strange, because even when the baby was at home and sick, no one whispered or walked in any special way.

After she had washed, Molly sat meekly down at the breakfast table. She had been arguing with Mama. She had wanted to stay home from school, so she could be near news of the baby, but Mama had said, "Nothing doing, when you come home I'll tell you the news."

Molly's finger hurt, but she didn't want to blow on it, or call attention to it. Mama brought over the hot Ovaltine and poured her a cup.

"You want some too?" Mama asked Joey.

Joey was finishing a glass of milk and a chocolate doughnut. He shook his head; then he wiped his mouth and got up and left for school. Papa sat drumming on the table with his fingers. He and Mama had decided that Mama would go to the hospital in the morning, and then again with Papa when he came home from work.

Mama pushed a buttered roll in front of Molly. "Eat something," she said.

Molly didn't feel like eating. But she didn't feel like arguing anymore either. She took the roll and ate half of it. Then she got her schoolbag and went out.

Solly was just a few steps ahead of her. Another time, she would have run to catch up with him. But today she didn't. She was too troubled to talk to anyone. She slowed down and let him get well ahead of her. Then she walked on to school.

As she entered the classroom she saw that Beverly was back. *If only it were Tsippi*, Molly thought, glancing longingly at her best friend's empty seat. She sat down sadly.

Beverly slid over and whispered in her ear. Molly heard something about a cousin and a dog, then put her hands over her ears and looked away.

The bell rang, and Miss McCabe stood up.

"Class," she said, "there seems to be an epidemic going around the school."

Molly's heart tightened. Did Tsippi have more than the grippe? Was she going to die? Was she already dead? Molly made up her mind. Germs or no germs, she would go to Tsippi's house after school. She could talk to her through the door.

"A lot of children have lice," Miss McCabe said.

"Oh, nits," the class groaned.

Molly shuddered. Ugh! She hadn't thought of anything like that. But at least it was better than infantile paralysis or scarlet fever or things like that.

"It's nothing to be ashamed of," Miss McCabe said. "But they are very catching, and we have to stop them where we can so they won't spread."

She had no sooner finished speaking when the door opened and the nurse came in.

The very sight of her made Molly nervous. What if she

had nits? What if she were sent home? She would die of shame.

The nurse nodded to Miss McCabe and went to the windows. She had a long, thin stick in her hand.

"Children," she said, "we're checking everyone in the school. It's no crime if you have lice. But if you have them, go right home and tell your mother to wash your hair in kerosine and comb it with a fine-tooth comb. Tell your mother you're not to come back to school until your head is clean."

Beverly leaned over to Molly. "Providence has nits. I saw them. They walk all over her head."

Molly shuddered.

"Molly, no whispering!" Miss McCabe called.

Molly made a face at her seatmate and looked away in disgust.

"The row near the wardrobe, form a line and come up to be examined," the nurse said. "Part your hair and hold it, so I can see. Keep your head away from your neighbor. Lice are catching."

Out of the corner of her eye, Molly saw Beverly give her a long, suspicious glance and slide to the extreme end of the seat, as if she were afraid to get too close.

Molly turned and glared at her, then faced the window to watch the first row being examined. The nurse looked in each part. Sometimes she used the stick to make another part in someone's hair. One boy and one girl were sent home. Then more kids went up. Then Providence's row. Molly was glad to see Providence go right back to her seat. She turned to Beverly. "That's how much you know," she said, and made a face.

Suddenly Molly's row stood up. She was in a sweat when her turn came. Her heart sank as she held her hair parted and bent so the nurse could look inside. She was overjoyed when the nurse told her to go back to her seat.

A few of the children in her row were sent home, and Molly felt the need to say something. She turned to Norma, the girl who sat behind her, and said how glad she was that she had been sent back to her seat. Norma was too. When Molly faced forward again, she saw Beverly rushing out of the room.

Serves her right, Molly thought, feeling half glad. Suddenly she was worried. Beverly's head was practically on top of her before. She could have caught Beverly's nits. They were new, and the nurse wouldn't be able to see them yet. Molly shivered. She thought she felt things crawling on her head.

Molly decided she would stay home in the afternoon, no matter what her mother said. And she would wash her hair in kerosine, just to be on the safe side. The way her luck was going, she couldn't be too careful. She felt like staying home anyhow and being close to the family, with Yaaki in the hospital.

When the nurse left, Miss McCabe took up fractions. Molly couldn't do fractions even when she had a clear mind. Miss McCabe knew it and never called on her. Today, Molly's mind was full of worries as she thought of Yaaki, lying in a dark hospital room, alone and scared; Tsippi, with a thermometer in her mouth; Hanna Gittel, crying because she had lost her ring.

Molly looked at her finger in disgust. Everything, all her misfortunes, seemed to have started on the day she had found the ring. She thought bitterly of Bette Davis for a moment, knowing it wasn't fair.

At last the bell rang for lunch.

Molly hurried across the street to Tsippi's house, went up two flights, and knocked on her friend's door. She shifted her schoolbag to her left hand, so the ring wouldn't show.

Tsippi's stepmother came to the door. A little rolled-up cigarette hung from the side of her mouth. Molly was always surprised by Mrs. Shaeffer. She was a greenhorn too, like Mama. And her accent was even worse than Mama's. But she smoked and did other modern things.

"Hello, Molly," Mrs. Shaeffer said out of the empty side of her mouth.

Molly saw Tsippi's form briefly and tried to look behind Mrs. Shaeffer. "I was wondering how Tsippi was feeling. . . ."

Tsippi came rushing over. She wasn't wearing her glasses and she crinkled her eyes as she smiled at Molly. Molly was glad to see her friend.

Mrs. Shaeffer pushed Tsippi back from the door. "Don't stand in a draft," she said.

"I'm better," Tsippi said from behind her stepmother. "No more fever."

"No more fever, but I'm keeping her in a few more days yet," Mrs. Shaeffer said.

"When will she come back to school?" Molly said, feeling strange talking about Tsippi when there she was.

"Maybe Friday. . . ."

Molly moved to the side so she could see Tsippi better. "Yaaki's in the hospital," she said.

"Ooooo!" Tsippi cried, covering her mouth with her hand.

"You better go, Molly, you'll see her Friday. There's a draft with the door open. I don't want her to get sick again."

"Good-bye," Molly called as the door closed in front of her.

Mama was in the kitchen, cooking, when Molly came in. Rebecca was sitting at the table, drawing in her coloring book. Molly put down her books and glanced at the empty crib in the living room.

"Did you go to the hospital, Ma?" she asked.

"I just came back," Mama said, stirring a pot on the stove. "He's a little better." She took a taste from the pot with a big spoon.

Molly wondered what "a little better" meant as she sliced bananas for lunch. It wasn't as good as better, or fine. She studied her mother's face. Mama had looked worse last night. Molly took it as a good sign and felt a little reassured. As she took three bowls out of the cupboard, she noticed that Rebecca's mouth was red.

"Ma, did you leave Rebecca with Mrs. Chiodo?" she asked.

Mama and Rebecca both looked up.

"How did you know?" Mama asked.

Molly shrugged. "I just did." She wiped her mouth with her tongue, showing Rebecca how she knew, and Rebecca did likewise.

"Ma," Molly said, "I'm not going back to school this afternoon. I have to wash my hair in kerosine."

"We'll see," Mama said. "What's kerosine?"

"There's an epidemic in school," Molly said. "Lice. You have to wash your hair with kerosine when you have them."

Mama looked at her. "You have lice?"

"I don't know. But Beverly does, and they're very catching."

"Can't you wash your hair later, after school?" Mama asked as she filled three glasses with milk.

"Ma, I don't want to take any chances," Molly said. "Beverly sits right next to me and she's always falling all over me with her head. The nurse said they're catching."

"What subjects have you got this afternoon?" Mama asked.

"Gym and assembly," Molly said, knowing Mama would give in.

Mama added sour cream to the bananas. "What's kerosine?" she asked. "Where do you buy it?"

"I don't know," Molly said.

"Let's eat now—I'm hungry," Mama said, sitting down. She took Rebecca's coloring book away and slid a bowl before her. Molly sat down and they all ate. When they were through Mama went to the courtyard window.

"Mrs. Baumfeld!" she called upstairs.

Mrs. Baumfeld came to the window.

"What's kerosine?" Mama asked.

"Kerosine?" Mrs. Baumfeld repeated. "I don't know."

Mrs. Marcus came to the window below and hung out a set of long underwear. "I know what kerosine is," she said, "from when my daughter was in elementary school."

Molly wondered what was going to happen. Mama didn't like Mrs. Marcus. She didn't speak to her. Molly watched the underwear dance across the yard as Mrs. Marcus moved the line forward.

"So—where does a person buy it?" Mama asked in a tight voice.

"In a hardware store."

The underwear was joined by a man's shirt.

"Thank you," Mama said. She made a face as she came away from the window. She took some coins out of her pocketbook and gave them to Molly.

"Take Rebecca, and go to the hardwerry store on Thirteenth Avenue. You know where it is?"

Molly nodded. "Sure, it's near Julie."

"I'll have a cuppy coffee, then I'll go to the hospital again. I have to see him. Such a little baby . . . When I come back, we'll wash your hair."

Rebecca jumped down from the chair and went to the door. She stood there waiting, the rag in her mouth.

"Ma," Molly said, "is Rebecca ever going to stop sucking on that thing?"

"How should I know? Ask her," Mama said, pouring herself some coffee and sitting down at the table.

Rebecca took the rag out of her mouth, placed it on the shelf of the cupboard, then went to the door and opened it.

Mama and Molly glanced at each other.

"Don't lose the money," Mama said.

Molly held up her clenched fist. "I won't."

The hardware store was full of customers. The owner was in back with some of them. Molly and Rebecca stayed in front, where there were boxes full of screws and nails and other things to see. Molly had picked up a round steel ball and stood looking at it.

"Hi, Molly," she heard someone say.

When she turned, Hanna Gittel was standing before her. The shock nearly took Molly's breath away. Molly turned slowly to hide her left hand. "Hello," she said, aware that her voice sounded funny.

"Do you live around here?" Hanna Gittel asked.

"Around the corner, on Forty-third Street," Molly said, watching Rebecca walk to the back. Molly thought her brain was on fire, the way she felt. She couldn't, she just couldn't bring herself to mention the ring while it was still on her finger.

"I live on Forty-second Street, over the butcher," Hanna Gittel said.

"Not near Julie?" Molly asked, forcing herself to speak.

"No, she comes to the butcher for her mother, so I see her. But she doesn't know me."

Some people were leaving, and girls stepped out of the way to let them pass. Molly kept her right side to Hanna Gittel. She thought Hanna would leave when the door was opened, but she stayed on.

"I came in to buy oil for my mother's wheelchair," Hanna Gittel said. "The wheels squeak."

"Wheelchair?" Molly asked.

"She can't walk yet," Hanna Gittel said. "The Nazis broke her legs when we left Poland. The doctors here are trying to fix them."

Much as Molly would have liked Hanna Gittel to leave, her heart went out to her and she wanted to hear more. "How— Who takes care of the house?" she asked, despite herself.

"I clean," Hanna Gittel said. "My mother cooks. My uncle lives with us. He helps too."

Molly remembered thinking once that the kids in Hebrew school were drips. It made her ashamed.

Rebecca came over and pulled Molly by the sleeve. "The man wants to know what you want to buy," she said. "I can't say it."

"I have to go anyhow," Hanna Gittel said, opening the door.

"Are you going to *shul* on Yom Kippur?" Molly asked.

Hanna Gittel nodded.

"So I'll see you there," Molly said. *Maybe before*, she thought, *if I get the ring off.*

Mama was not yet home when Molly and Rebecca got back. Molly felt restless and cranky. She had had enough to worry about, with Yaaki in the hospital and the ring and Hanna Gittel. Now she had Hanna Gittel's mother's legs to worry about too. She didn't want to think. Selma had bought the *Daily News* yesterday and left the jokes behind. Molly had already read them. She wanted to read them again, and got them from Joey's room and sat down on the couch with them. As she read, she worked the ring, trying to get it off.

Rebecca came up to her. "Read to me, Molly."

Molly didn't want to be bothered. "I don't feel like it. Draw in your coloring book."

"I want you to read to me," Rebecca insisted.

Molly waved her away and went on reading.

Rebecca hopped up on the couch and sat down next to her. "I have a secret to tell you, Molly," she said.

Molly looked at her.

"Remember when I ate in Mrs. Chiodo's house that time?" Rebecca asked.

Molly nodded, wondering which time she meant.

"I lied," Rebecca said. "I did eat the meatball. That's why Yaaki got sick. The meatball wasn't kosher. It was a sin. That's why God punished me."

Molly could hardly speak. She stared at Rebecca, marveling that her sister's thought had been so like her own. A moment later, when she recovered, she almost had to laugh. *A meatball*, she thought, considering her own much larger sin.

"That's not why," she said. "A meatball hardly counts. It's a tiny sin. God doesn't pay attention to such sins, only Mama and Papa do. God would never do anything like that for such a tiny sin."

She could see her words had made Rebecca feel better.

Rebecca went into the other room and came back with Molly's library book. "You want me to read *you* a story?"

"Okay," Molly said, hoping that would give Rebecca something to do and she would leave her alone.

"Once there was a Sinbad the Sailor," Rebecca began.

As Rebecca spoke on, Molly worked the ring. Her finger was tender and she had to go easy. After a while, Rebecca's words reached her ear and she couldn't help but listen. Rebecca turned the page and continued a story, repeating phrases from "Snow White," *Little Women*, "Pinocchio," and other tales that Molly had read to her, and it almost sounded as if she *were* reading.

"It looks like a library in here," Mama said.

"Ma!" Molly called, surprised. She hadn't heard her come in. "How is Yaaki?"

"His color is better. He even stood up a little," Mama said.

Molly weighed Mama's report. The words were better than earlier. Her voice wasn't as tight. And her face seemed less worried. Molly flashed a quick thank you to God. "Can I go to the hospital, Ma?"

"They won't let you in—you're too young. You have to be twelve," Mama said.

Molly was secretly glad. She wanted very much to see the baby. But she was afraid of a hospital. She got up to get the kerosine.

"Wait a minute, I'm not finished," Rebecca said.

"Excuse me," Molly said, sitting down again.

Rebecca turned the page. "And then the real mother came in and took the princess and kissed her and put her in Goldilocks's chair, and kissed her good night." Molly looked at her. "Are you finished?"

"That's the end," Rebecca said.

Molly got up again. "A very nice story," she said, reminding herself of Miss McCabe. "Let's wash my hair, Ma. Okay?" she asked.

"I'll just peel some potatoes for supper," Mama said.

Mama washed Molly's hair in the bathroom sink and Rebecca leaned against the bathtub, holding her nose and complaining about the smell. Molly didn't like the smell either. But the way it burned her head was even worse. When it was all over Molly went into the living room to read, and work on the ring. After a while she forgot about the ring and read on. *That's what's so wonderful about a book,* she thought as she turned the page. *You forget your troubles and watch somebody else's life.*

"Molly!" Mama called from the kitchen. "Turn on the radio, the good programs are coming on."

Molly turned the dial and let the radio warm up. When Mama and Rebecca sat down in the living room, she took hold of the loose wire in back to bring up the sound, and they all sat listening to *Life Can Be Beautiful*.

The front door opened and Joey came in. "What stinks in here?" he said, dropping his books on the kitchen table. "Ma, I'm going to the hospital," he called, and ran out again.

The program was still on when Papa came home. He made himself a glass of tea, then went into the bathroom to shave. Molly had heard him mention his Jewish War Veterans meeting later that night.

Mama got up. "I know how it's going to end already," she said, going into the kitchen.

Molly knew that Mama had gone to tell Papa how the baby was. Molly didn't have patience to sit there and listen either. Chichi was always almost going to do something but she never did it. Molly went into the kitchen and sat down at the table. Mama took a bowl out of the closet and began grating potatoes.

"We'll have potato *latkes* for supper," Mama said.

Rebecca turned off the radio and came walking into the kitchen.

"The man went back to Chicago," she said.

"I'm glad," Mama said. "He was no good."

"But she loved him."

"He was a bum. He didn't want to work. He wanted her to support him."

"But she loved him," Rebecca repeated.

Papa stepped out into the kitchen from the bathroom,

his face half covered with shaving cream. "What is this, Laya?" he said. "You're arguing with a child?"

"I'm not arguing," Mama said.

"I'm not a child," Rebecca said.

"No? What are you?" Papa asked.

"A little girl," Rebecca said.

Papa picked her up and kissed her.

"Don't," Rebecca said, wiping the shaving cream from her face.

Papa put her down and sniffed at the air. "What's that smell? It's in the bathroom too," he said.

"I'll tell you later," Mama said. "Meanwhile, finish shaving. I need a few things from the store."

Molly was glad Mama didn't say anything. She didn't feel like explaining. She didn't feel like talking.

Joey came home from the hospital, and they all sat down to eat. After supper Mama and Papa went to the hospital and the children went into the living room to listen to the radio. They glanced at the empty crib. It was a terrible sight.

"I'll hold the wire," Joey said, taking the seat closest to the radio.

Molly felt a twinge of guilt as *The Shadow* came on and said, "Who knows what evil lurks in the hearts of men?" Then she sat listening, glad it was a mystery and took her attention away from herself. Rebecca got up in the middle of the program and said she was going to sleep.

Molly realized suddenly that she hadn't seen Rebecca with the sucking rag since she had laid it aside.

"I think she stopped sucking on the rag," she whispered to Joey.

"Shh," he said, adding, "It's about time."

Molly found her thoughts drifting when *The Shadow* was over and Joey turned on Amos 'n' Andy. Usually she liked that program. But there was too much talking in it for her tonight.

"I'm tired too," she said, getting up.

"You're not going to wait for the end?" Joey asked.

"I'm too tired."

"I'll just listen to this, then do my homework," Joey said.

Molly went into the bathroom to wash up. While she was in there she parted her hair in the center and tried to look at her part in the mirror but couldn't. Then she made a part near her ear. She couldn't see too much. She hoped there was nothing to see.

She walked past Joey and went into her room and gently got into bed so as not to wake Rebecca.

Tired as she was, she could not fall asleep. She heard when Joey turned the radio off, when Mama and Papa came home, when Papa opened the couch in the living room before going off to his meeting. She pretended to be asleep when Mama peeked into the room.

She lay facedown, thinking. God had helped. Things seemed to be a little better. She wanted to talk to God and turned over on her back so as not to be disrespectful.

"Dear God," she said, "thanks for making Yaaki's color better. Please make him all better, so my whole family can be happy again. And God, I want to give the ring back like anything, you know I do, so Hanna Gittel can be happy too." Molly thought of Hanna Gittel's mother in a wheelchair and winced. "Please help me get it off, God."

The only thought that Molly could find in her head that she liked was that she would be seeing Tsippi on Friday. "Tsippi, I miss you so much," she called to her absent friend.

Molly wished she had someone to be close to. But there was only Rebecca. She glanced over at her sister's sturdy little figure. Rebecca was better than nothing, so she inched over and lightly, lightly dropped her arm over Rebecca.

After a while she fell asleep.

8

MOLLY IS FORGIVEN

The week passed slowly for Molly. Each day was the same as the one before. The baby seemed to be better. Mama and Papa both said so, and everyone seemed more cheerful in general. According to Joey, the doctors liked Yaaki best because he never cried.

But her other problem was still with her, and suddenly it was Thursday and the ring was still clamped around her finger. After supper, as everyone listened to the radio, she spent the whole time trying to pull it off. And when she went to bed she tried. And after Rebecca fell asleep and there was no one to see, she got out of bed and went to the window to pray. And standing there in the sight of God she prayed that when she woke in the morning the ring would be off.

Until she fell asleep, she pulled and tugged. But when she got up in the morning the ring was in its usual place and her finger was swollen double.

Molly was numb as she dressed and tiptoed out of the room. Joey was on his way out, and she caught sight of his back as she sat down at the breakfast table. Mama and Papa were drinking coffee. Her finger was purple and it throbbed. She hid it in her lap.

"You're not eating?" Mama said.

"I'm not hungry."

"You don't have to be hungry to eat," Mama said.

Molly bit into a roll and took a sip of cocoa.

Papa reached for a piece of bread and buttered it. "You know what?" he said, talking to Mama. "We're closing early today, for Yom Kippur. Why should I go in for a few hours? It doesn't pay. It's not worth the carfare. I'll stay home and help. Later, we'll go to the hospital together."

"Fine by me," Mama said. "When you go out to call the boss, get doughnuts. Joey ate the last one."

Molly ate what she could, then went into the bathroom. The cold water made her finger feel better, and she opened the faucet and put her finger under it. She leaned over the sink watching the water rush down over her purple and swollen finger.

"Molly!" she heard Mama call through the door. "Tsippi is here."

Molly could have cried. She had almost forgotten about Tsippi. She shut off the water and went out, keeping her hand down.

"Hi," she said, glad to see her friend again. "Are you all better?"

Tsippi smiled and pushed her glasses up on her nose. "I'm better, but look what my mother made me wear, like it's the North Pole," she said, indicating a hat, coat, muffler, and mittens.

Molly smiled. "I'll go get my books."

She went into her room for them, and when she came out she found Tsippi in the living room, leaning over the empty crib, looking inside.

"It's the first time I saw him not there," Tsippi said. "He'll be home soon, watch and see," she added after a moment.

[107]

Molly could tell from the way Tsippi's nose twitched that she was trying not to cry. It made Molly want to cry too. "Let's go," she said, blinking away her tears and leading the way through the kitchen. "So long," she called to her parents from the door.

Outside, Molly let Tsippi do the talking. She walked along in silence, bearing the pain. Tsippi was telling her how awful it was, being cooped up at home so long. Molly could hardly listen. All she could think of was the pain in her finger.

At the corner, the light turned red and they stopped to wait.

"My stepmother made me promise I wouldn't call for you today—she said I was still weak. I had to stand in the muffler and all my clothes in the heat and promise. She was making me sick again."

Molly tried to smile as they crossed the street.

"This is the first time I ever broke a promise to her," Tsippi said.

Again Molly tried to smile. She couldn't help wondering, what was a broken promise compared to what she had done? Even so, it was something. The fact that Tsippi admitted it made it easier for Molly to talk. She just had to say something or she was afraid she might explode.

"Look at my finger," she said as they entered the school yard. "It's killing me."

"Ooooo!" Tsippi said, stopping to look. "Your finger is all swollen."

Molly promised herself to tell Tsippi all about it sometime. But not today.

"Yoo-hoo! Molly! Tsippi!" Julie called from across the school yard. She and the two Naomis had entered from the other side. They all waved. Molly and Tsippi waved back and went inside. Molly kept stopping to blow on her finger as they went up the stairs.

"Come on," Tsippi said when they got to the first floor. "We better tell Miss McCabe." She took Molly's schoolbag from her and held her hand.

Molly hurried along after her, happy that something was going to happen, she almost didn't care what. She couldn't keep it to herself anymore. She needed help.

"Look, Miss McCabe, look at Molly's finger," Tsippi said, shoving Molly forward.

Miss McCabe put her paper down and looked at Molly's hand. "Does your mother know?" she asked.

Molly shook her head, realizing it made Mama seem like a bad mother. Tears began to form in her eyes and she looked away, hoping her mother would forgive her.

"I think we should go see Mr. Brooke," Miss McCabe said.

Tsippi had been standing by. "I'll see you later," she whispered and took her seat.

Molly wiped away her tears and tried to smile. She didn't want anyone in class calling her a crybaby either.

"Class," Miss McCabe said, "take out your readers and read a story silently to yourselves. Any story. Those who finish before I get back, turn to page fourteen and memorize the first stanza of *Hiawatha*."

"By Henry Wadsworth Longfellow," Molly said under her breath, as if she had been asked the question.

"Providence," Miss McCabe called, "I'm appointing you monitor. Come to the front and keep order while I'm gone."

Providence ran to the front of the room.

Miss McCabe headed for the door and Molly glanced at Tsippi as she followed the teacher out. Once she set foot in the hall, Molly couldn't stop herself from crying. She cried and cried. Through tear-filled eyes, she followed Miss McCabe down the stairs. The next thing she knew, she was in the principal's office, sitting on a chair near the window. When she looked up, she saw Mr. Brooke standing over her.

He took her hand. "We've got to get that off."

"It's—stuck. It—won't come off," Molly said through her tears.

"We'll find a way," he said, and went to the phone on his desk.

Miss McCabe smiled at her. Molly made an effort to smile back, then glanced away and looked at the ring. It had brought nothing but trouble. "Finders weepers," she thought sadly.

Mr. Brooke hung up the phone. "We're going to cut it off," he said.

Molly grabbed her hand. "My finger?" she cried.

Mr. Brooke and Miss McCabe laughed. "No, just the ring," he said. "I hope it isn't valuable."

"Oh, no," Molly said quickly, so he wouldn't change his mind.

"Your mother won't care?"

Molly shook her head. "It's just a piece of junk," she said, remembering the phrase from someplace.

"Good," Mr. Brooke said. "Tony is on the way up with his toolbox. He'll have it off in a jiffy."

Miss McCabe went to the door. "You don't need me anymore, Elton, do you?"

"No, Mary Katherine," Mr. Brooke said. "Molly and I will be fine."

Molly glanced at them, wondering if they were boy and girlfriend.

"Come back to class when you're through," Miss McCabe told Molly from the door.

"If I'm alive," Molly said tearfully.

"You will be," Miss McCabe said, and left.

A moment later Tony, the janitor, was standing beside Molly with his toolbox. "I'll have it off in a second," he said. He took a snipper out of his box. Mr. Brooke stood by, watching.

"Hold still, it won't hurt," Tony said, taking Molly's hand.

Molly looked away, as if she were getting a shot.

SNIP!

"There," Tony said, handing her the ring. "Too bad we had to make a cut in it, but they can probably seal it together."

Molly stared at the ring. Was it really off? A feeling like joy exploded inside her and she began to cry.

"Why are you crying?" Mr. Brooke asked. "It doesn't hurt, does it?"

Molly shook her head. Her finger still hurt some, but that wasn't it. She was crying because of the relief.

"Thanks, Tony," Mr. Brooke said as the man went to the door. "Can you get back to class alone, Molly?" he asked. "Or shall I send one of the boys with you?"

Molly was shocked. She wasn't finished crying yet.

How could he ask her that? She pulled herself together and decided to go back alone. Bravery was like a good deed. And she wanted to add all the good deeds she could think of to her record.

Grasping the ring, she stood up. "I can go alone," she said, hoping God was watching.

It seemed to her, as she went up the stairs, that she had been gone a long time. She wondered how much she had missed. Everyone turned to look at her as she entered the room.

"Eyes front!" Miss M꜀Cabe called.

Molly glanced at Tsippi as she slid into her seat and dropped the ring into her schoolbag. She was so relieved to be rid of it she would have hugged Beverly if she had been there.

Miss M꜀Cabe went to the board. "Class, you have all heard of Germany, Austria, Italy, and France from the war stories," she said. She picked up her pointer and rolled a map down over the board. "Switzerland is this little green bit over here," she said, pointing, "under Germany and Austria, above Italy, and next to France. Switzerland is neutral. She is not in the war."

At last, Molly thought. *No more Peru.*

As Miss M꜀Cabe spoke on, Molly's thoughts turned to the problems that still faced her. She lowered her eyes and gently—her finger still hurt—folded her hands on the desk.

"Dear God," she said under her breath. "The ring is off, as you can see." She released the finger and showed it. "I'm sorry they had to cut it, but I couldn't help it. Tony said it could be sealed together. And tonight Hanna Gittel will have her ring back, so everything is better. Except, God, for Yaaki. He's still in the hospital. Please make him well and let everything be better. Hurry!" She paused, then added, "If you can," not wanting to sound too demanding.

". . . cuckoo clocks," she heard Miss McCabe say when she looked up. The class laughed. Then the bell rang for lunch.

Everyone jumped up.

"Not so fast," Miss McCabe said. "Does anyone know what day this is?"

"Tonight starts Yom Kippur," several voices rang out.

"Cor-rect. It begins at sundown and the Jewish children will not be back after lunch. Yom Kippur in English means Day of Atonement," she continued. "To atone means regret, or feel sorry about. On this holiday they regret their sins and pray to be forgiven."

Molly's spirits began to sink again when she realized how much she had to be forgiven for. Miss McCabe had surprised her again. She wondered if the teacher was half Jewish.

"I'll see the rest of you after lunch," Miss McCabe said. "If there are any sinners among you, you can atone right here," she added, pulling her mouth over to the side in a smile.

Molly smiled, to let the teacher know she got the joke.

As everyone got up to leave, Miss McCabe beckoned to Molly.

"Well," she said, taking Molly's hand, "that must feel a lot better."

Molly was thrilled to have Miss McCabe holding her hand. "It does," she said, blushing. She loved the teacher deeply at that moment and didn't know what to do. "Thanks," she added, embarrassed, and ran out into the hall, where Tsippi was waiting for her.

"Is your finger better?" Tsippi asked.

Molly nodded.

"Where's the ring?"

Molly took it out of her schoolbag and held it up.

"It has a slit at the bottom," Tsippi said. "Your mother won't be mad?"

"Naaa," Molly said. She did not want to say too much. She did not want to lie either, now that everything was right again.

They paused at the school yard gate.

"Are you going to *shul* tonight?" Tsippi asked.

Molly nodded. "We're all going."

"I wish I could go. But my parents don't believe in religion. All they care about is labor unions and workers and strikes."

Molly was secretly glad Tsippi would not be going to the synagogue. She did not want Tsippi and Hanna Gittel to meet, not at this time.

"It's not so hot," she said, making light of it.

"Are you going to fast?" Tsippi asked.

It had never occurred to Molly to fast. Children weren't supposed to. But it would count as a good deed if she did fast.

"If my mother lets me," she said.

"So long," Tsippi said over her shoulder as she crossed the street.

Molly waved good-bye and ran home. She made up

her mind to wear her dusty-pink dress to the synagogue. She didn't care if it was too tight. She liked it. Besides, it had a pocket.

"Molly! Good news!" Mama cried as Molly opened the door. "Yaaki is better. The doctor said we could bring him home Sunday."

Molly's heart exploded with joy. She couldn't believe how quickly God had acted. Under her breath she sent God a message of thanks.

"Ma," she said, "I want to fast for Yom Kippur."

Papa called from the bathroom, where he was shaving, "Children don't have to fast."

"I know, but I want to anyhow," Molly answered. "Ask Mama."

"Fast if you want," Mama said. "There's food if you'll get hungry." Joey was doing his homework at the kitchen table. "Are you fasting too?" Mama asked.

"I wasn't going to," Joey said, scribbling away. "But if she fasts, I'll fast."

Mama laughed. "We'll see how long the fast lasts. Meanwhile let's sit down and eat. Rebecca!" she called.

Rebecca came in holding her little plastic doll.

"What's the dolly's name?" Molly asked, feeling playful.

"Don't call her 'dolly'—she's not a baby. Her name is Ruthie," Rebecca said.

Molly shrugged and went to put her schoolbag in her room. Then she joined everyone at the table.

Later, she got out her library book and sat down on the couch.

"Rebecca, want me to read to you?" she called.

Rebecca came in and hopped up on the couch. She put her little plastic doll down beside her. Molly pulled her sister closer and began to read aloud from the Bobbsey Twins.

"Where's the ring?" Rebecca asked suddenly.

Molly was startled. She didn't know what to say. "Gone," she answered. She wondered what her sister was thinking. She didn't really want to know. She was only glad Rebecca said nothing more. Gratefully, she continued. " 'The clown picked up the basket where the envelope was hidden and handed it to Freddie and Flossie with it,' " she said, reading on.

"Molly!" Mama called. "Get dressed."

"That's the end of the chapter," Molly said. As she looked at her sister, she felt a great outpouring of love for her. She felt like putting her arms around her.

"If I hug you, will you let me?" she asked.

Rebecca hopped down from the couch and stood with her arms at her sides. "You can hug me," she said.

Molly gave her a squeeze, then they both went into the kitchen. Joey was showing off his new suit.

"You look nice, Joey," Molly said, looking at him admiringly.

"Like a regular pointy," Mama said.

Joey laughed.

"Not pointy, Ma, *sharpie!*" Molly said.

"It's the same thing," Mama said. She led Rebecca to the sink and washed her face. "Come on, Molly, get dressed. You'll wear the brown taffeta, no?"

"That ugly dress. I'm going to wear my dusty pink, I don't care if it is too tight," Molly said.

[117]

"I don't care what you wear, only get dressed. We have to go," Mama said.

Molly went into the bedroom and changed into her dusty pink. She looked at herself in the mirror. "The lady in pink . . ." she sang, snapping her fingers over her head. Then she took the ring out of her schoolbag and put it in her pocket. Finding herself alone, she went up to the window to talk to God. She opened the window, so there'd be no interference.

She looked up at the sky. "Thank you, God," she said.

"Molly!" Mama called.

"God, I'm going to *shul* tonight, and tomorrow too. And I'm going to fast even though I don't have to." Something like doubt rose up in her mind and she chased it away. "Please God, let my good deeds wash away my sins and bless me for the new year and bless Yaaki and my whole family and Hanna Gittel and her mother too."

"Molly!" Mama called again.

"Why is it so cold in here?" Molly heard Papa ask.

"Molly's talking to God with the window open," Joey said.

Molly wondered how he knew. "Thanks for everything, God. I mean it," she said, and ran into the kitchen where everyone was waiting for her.

On the walk to the synagogue, Molly found herself wondering how Hanna Gittel would react. What if she didn't believe Molly's story? What if she started to yell because of the cut? Or cry?

At the synagogue, Molly, Mama, and Rebecca went upstairs, to the women's section. Molly glanced around and didn't see Hanna Gittel, and went back downstairs to stand near the door. From there she could look into the men's section. Papa was in a prayer shawl. Joey was with him. A man was talking to them.

When she faced the street again she saw Hanna Gittel. She was walking beside a wheelchair. A man who had to be her uncle was pushing it. Molly watched as the uncle and another man lifted the chair and carried it up the steps. Molly's heart was pounding as the uncle rolled the chair inside and Hanna Gittel came toward her.

"Hi," Molly said.

"Oh, hi," Hanna Gittel answered. "I didn't see you."

"My—my mother and sister are upstairs in the balcony," Molly said, not knowing how to begin.

"I sit with my mother in the men's section," Hanna Gittel said. "It's too hard to carry the wheelchair up all the stairs."

Molly took the ring out of her pocket. Her heart was racing. "I heard you tell your friend in *shul* that time you lost your ring. Is this it?"

Hanna Gittel's eyes widened and she clapped her hands together. "Where did you find it?" she asked, taking it.

Molly had rehearsed. "On Forty-third Street, in the gutter, near the Chinese laundry, before, when I went shopping for my mother." Molly was about to bring up the cut and say that Tony said it could be sealed together, but she caught herself in time.

"It's got a cut in it," Hanna Gittel said dreamily. "That's all right. They can fix it. My father gave it to me when I was little," she added. She put it on the edge of her finger. "It was on a chain on my neck. I can't wear it no more. It's too small." She stood smiling at the ring.

Molly looked away. In the synagogue, the rabbi, in his white robes, was taking the Torah out of the ark and the men had stood up to pray.

"My mother's waiting for me," Molly said, heading for the stairs.

Hanna Gittel nodded and went inside.

All around Molly, voices were raised in prayer as she ran up to the balcony. Mama and Rebecca moved over to make room for her. She squeezed in beside them. She swore, as she stood between Mama and another lady, that she would never lie again. It wasn't worth it. Things only got worse and worse. She knew she would feel ashamed whenever she thought of the ring. But for now her misery was over and her heart was bursting with joy. There was a song she always sang when she felt that good. She thought of it as her happiness song. She glanced at Mama, glanced at the lady, then, hoping it wasn't a sin, she pressed her lips together and sang joyously inside her head:

I should worry, I should care
I should marry a millionaire.